GETTING SMART

Look for these other books about
The Practically Popular Crowd:

Wanting More
Pretty Enough
Keeping Secrets

THE PRACTICALLY POPULAR CROWD

GETTING SMART

Meg F. Schneider

AN
APPLE
PAPERBACK

SCHOLASTIC INC.
New York Toronto London Auckland Sydney

No part of this publication may be reproduced in whole or in part, or stored in a retrieval system, or transmitted in any form or by any means, electronic, mechanical, photocopying, recording, or otherwise, without written permission of the publisher. For information regarding permission, write to Scholastic Inc., 730 Broadway, New York, NY 10003.

ISBN 0-590-45478-1

12 11 10 9 8 7 6 5 4 3 2 1   3 4 5 6 7 8/9

Printed in the U.S.A.   40

First Scholastic printing, May 1993

To the Calhoun School

Prologue

Alexa stood in stunned silence, watching Rebecca Lake.

Who was this girl? How dare she behave this way?

Alexa whipped out a small mirror from her shoulder bag and checked her reflection. It was lovely. But, still . . .

She watched as Rebecca made her way around the room, smiling at everyone. Greeting everyone. As if they were her people. Her fans. Her most trusted confidantes.

As if she were Alexa.

Alexa tried to think. It was going to be a tough call.

Befriend Rebecca, or ignore Rebecca.

What was the safest thing to do?

Alexa frowned as James Wood gave Rebecca the once-over.

Or maybe just squash her. Like a bug.

GETTING SMART

1

Priscilla Levitt sat quietly in the empty school lunchroom, her notebook resting on the table before her.

It was so perplexing.

How could this have happened? To her? A D. She'd actually gotten a D. Twenty-five kids in her algebra class, and she'd managed to score lower than almost anyone.

Priscilla folded the quiz in half and tucked it into her notebook. Then she pulled from her pocket a bright-green plaid ribbon with gold edging and tied her long, wavy, golden-brown hair into a ponytail at the nape of her neck.

Junior high was certainly turning out to be a lot harder than seventh grade. Her grades had been good last year. She'd pulled B's in math and science, and history and English had always earned her A's. "Insightful" her teacher had said last year about her writing. "Original."

Somberly, Priscilla looked down at her notebook. Eighth grade was definitely not going well.

"Priscilla," a familiar warm voice broke into her thoughts.

She looked up to find Michelle Horne standing beside her with an expression of concern on her face. "You were out of Mrs. Simon's class so fast, I didn't even see you leave." She tucked her shoulder-length, dark wavy hair behind her ears. "Math isn't the be all and end all, you know."

Priscilla nodded and smiled brightly. "I know that," she said quickly. "Anyway, I didn't do THAT badly."

She couldn't help it. Her smile began to falter.

Her friends knew she'd been having a rough time. First there was algebra. And then that C on the science pop quiz. Followed by the B– on a book report.

Of course they'd all agreed it was just a passing thing. Priscilla had joked about being dumb, but she hadn't really believed that, and neither had they. Priscilla frowned. At least she hoped they hadn't.

"It's your art," Michelle continued supportively. "You're obsessed."

Priscilla nodded. "Isn't it terrible?" Yes, that had to be it.

Priscilla flipped her notebook open to an empty page and began doodling with a red felt-tip pen.

Michelle rested her hand on Priscilla's shoulder.

2

Priscilla cringed. She had too much pride for this.

If there was one thing she hated, it was pity.

"Michelle, I'm fine," Priscilla insisted. "Really." And she would be, too. If she didn't have friends who were doing well. Or brilliant parents. Or a brother who was so smart, he kept bringing notes home from his teachers suggesting he needed "enrichment" programs to address his unusual "gifts."

Priscilla began to pen the letter R in three dimensions.

And as if that wasn't enough.

Someone from the art period before hers had left behind a pencil sketch of a rosebud. It was utterly exquisite. Delicate. Sensitive. Something she'd have liked to have done herself. And in the corner were the initials R.L.

But she didn't know any talented R.L.'s. Just A.R.'s — Ann Rice. She was the only girl in school whose artistic skills compared to her own. Priscilla frowned again. One rival was enough.

Moments later, the soft whir of voices in the distance and pounding feet on the staircase grabbed her attention. She glanced up at Michelle.

It was time to change the subject. The last thing she wanted was a group guessing game called "How badly did Priscilla do?"

Especially if Adam Miller walked by. He was the brainiest, shyest guy in eighth grade, and for some reason she couldn't stop thinking about him. Not that he was gorgeous. He was more intense-looking than anything else. He wasn't much taller than Priscilla, but he had piercing gray eyes and a sweet smile. Lately she'd gotten the funniest feeling that he'd been eyeing her, too. . . .

Priscilla racked her brains for a topic. "Has Alexa landed that guy Mac yet?" she finally blurted out with forced merriment. She looked toward the lunchroom doors nervously. Adam could never know about her grades. Never.

"There you are," Margo Warner called out loudly as she burst through the swinging doors, heading straight for Priscilla. She walked over to the table and threw her books down. "Well, how did everyone do on the test? I got a B–. Not exactly my best showing." She paused. "Though it is about how I'd rate my figure. . . . " She frowned down at the oversized workshirt she'd thrown on to hide the extra pounds she just couldn't seem to shed.

"So, this is The Practically Flunked Crowd?" Vivienne Bennis asked as she descended upon the table with a broad grin. "You all look miserable! Cheer up! I have enough good grades to go around!"

"Oh, be quiet," Michelle snapped. "Honestly, Viv, do you have to be so conceited?"

Vivienne shook her head. "No. I'm sorry. I know I sound obnoxious. But I don't really mean

4

it that way." She turned to Priscilla with a serious look on her face. "The algebra test. No good?"

Priscilla smiled. "Not good. Not bad. But, hey, what do you expect? Can you draw?" She gave Vivienne's wavy blondish hair a playful tug. Vivienne's conceit never bothered her. It was just a cover-up for her insecurity about boys, and the fact that Vivienne didn't look much older than twelve.

Vivienne shrugged and began peering around the cafeteria.

Gina smiled. "I have a feeling you can do better than whatever you got, Priscilla. You seem pretty smart to me."

"I know," Priscilla nodded, less confidently than she'd intended. Then, again, no one from the crowd had ever gotten a D before. They all did very well in school. They were proud of that. They were proud of each other.

So far, anyway. The year was young.

Priscilla began drumming her fingers on her notebook.

Enough. She'd get it together. It was time to play the "artiste."

She stood up abruptly and pointed to her wide leather belt upon which she'd handpainted a paisley pattern in shades of green, purple, and pink. "You like?"

"Oh, it's gorgeous!" Gina cried out.

"Could you make me one?" Michelle sighed.

Priscilla nodded proudly.

"There she is!" Vivienne suddenly announced out of the blue.

"Who?" everyone said at once, whirling around to survey the bustling cafeteria.

"The new girl," Vivienne replied. She began waving frantically at a petite, dark-haired girl who stood tentatively in the doorway of the lunchroom, dressed in a snug, black, turtleneck dress, with gold star earrings dangling down almost to her shoulders. Priscilla could hardly believe her eyes. She was one of the most glamourous-looking girls Priscilla had ever seen.

With the possible exception of Alexa Craft.

"Over here," Vivienne called out over the din. Quickly she began weaving between the tables toward the new girl.

Priscilla looked dumbfounded at Michelle. "Who is she?"

"I don't know," Michelle shrugged. "I also don't know why Viv is acting like she's the Queen Bee. Hardly looks like her type."

"Or ours," Margo whispered. "She's some babe, as my brother would say. What would she want with us?" Immediately she pulled out a comb and ran it through the frizzy spot in her hair.

"That's Rebecca Lake," Gina volunteered. "This is her first day at school. She's in my homeroom. She seems awfully nice. And what do you mean 'what would she want with us?' We're cute!"

6

Priscilla's eyes traveled back to the girl who was now advancing on the table with a big friendly smile, her thick, super-dark, glossy hair bouncing about her shoulders.

So here she was. In all probability, Ms. R.L.

"Everyone, I'd like you to meet Rebecca Lake," Vivienne began, tucking her wavy, dark blonde hair behind her ears. "She just arrived from Michigan." She began nodding around the table. "This is Michelle, our therapist and flutist; Margo, our comedienne and politician; Gina, our athlete and occasional wild person; and Priscilla, our confident artiste!"

"Hi!" Rebecca smiled as she looked from girl to girl. "You're all so terrific-looking!" she sang out.

"We try!" Margo giggled as she sucked in her stomach.

"Goodness, we never thought of ourselves that way!" Gina exclaimed, obviously very pleased.

"You're not bad yourself," Michelle replied. "I love your earrings."

"And we're smart, too," Vivienne offered.

Rebecca grinned at Vivienne. "An A in algebra and cool-looking, too? You're something else. Do you think some of you could rub off on me? Please!?"

Vivienne, all aglow, simply looked around the table at her friends. "I think so . . . " she said softly.

Priscilla glanced around the same table with bewilderment.

Were they kidding?

Their smiles were so bright. So pleased. So earnest.

Did they really think this girl was for real?

A vision of the rosebud floated before her. Priscilla willed a friendly grin upon her face.

"Are you the R.L. who did that sketch of the rosebud I saw in the art room today?" she asked in as cordial a voice as she could muster.

Rebecca nodded. "Did you like it?"

"Very much," Priscilla nodded. "I did. You're talented."

"I heard you are, too," Rebecca continued. "Very talented, in fact. Vivienne here told me about each of you during a break. About how you have this kind of informal group where you share secrets and help each other. Kind of like a support group or something. And how you protect each other from that show-off who used to be your friend. You know. Alexa something." She smiled at Vivienne. "I was jealous just thinking about it. . . . "

For a moment, everyone was completely silent.

Vivienne shifted her weight uncomfortably from one foot to the other.

It was an unspoken given that the group was a private thing. They didn't discuss it in public because they had lots of other friends, too. They didn't want anyone feeling left out. But the group, the Crowd, was something special. Their meetings were between them and only them. Trust was critical. The Crowd wasn't a secret. Just very personal.

"It just kind of slipped out. . . . " Vivienne murmured.

Rebecca looked around the table. "Oh. Did I say something I shouldn't have? I wasn't trying to hint or anything. . . . "

"No, no," Margo assured her. "It's fine."

"Absolutely," Gina added. "No problem."

"Would you like to join us for lunch?" Michelle added.

"Please do!" Vivienne exclaimed.

"Are you sure you wouldn't mind? I don't want to intrude," Rebecca responded as she plunked down her books and bag before anyone had a chance to answer.

Priscilla looked away with annoyance.

"Stay!" Michelle insisted.

"We'd like you to," Gina agreed.

Priscilla pulled an apple from her book bag and began to chomp on it thoughtfully.

Rebecca Lake. What a name.

It sounded like some kind of Hollywood star.

Plastic. Unreal. Fake.

Priscilla sighed heavily as The Practically Popular Crowd fluttered busily, attentively, about Rebecca.

Something didn't feel right.

The question was, why was she the only one who felt it?

2

"So," Alexa began slowly on Wednesday afternoon as she turned in front of the full-length mirror affixed to her closet door. "I suppose you two think this Rebecca Lake is something. Huh?"

"Well, sure she's good-looking," Robin offered quickly. "Not like you, though." Nervously she ran a hand through her thick short curls, and pushed up the sleeves of her turquoise sweater.

Alexa smiled slightly. Robin said the nicest things. A little too often, in fact. Alexa took a deep breath, then turned to face Mona. "And you?" she asked as casually as she could manage. "What's your take?"

Mona hesitated.

Alexa quickly looked away and pretended to pull a piece of lint from her soft pink scoop-necked sweater. Darn Mona. She was doing it again. Reaching for the truth. On the one hand, it was so comforting, so reliable. On the other, it was such a drag.

"Actually, I think Rebecca is beautiful . . . in a dark, mysterious kind of way," Mona answered.

Alexa frowned. Funny how the truth was so rarely what she wanted to hear. She leaned into the mirror for a closer examination. Nope. Nothing mysterious there. Just a lot of blonde, curvy, good looks. She sighed and leaned back. That used to be just great. But not anymore. She could see it in the eyes of every boy in school. Dark and mysterious was definitely gaining on California blonde.

"Rebecca is very attractive," Alexa proclaimed glumly. She turned to study her two friends. A decision had to be made. "So what should we do?" She held both hands out. "I'm open to suggestions."

"Well, what do you mean?" Mona asked, completely mystified. "About what?"

"I mean what's our position?" Alexa continued flatly.

"I don't get it . . . " Robin responded.

Alexa shook her head. "You guys don't see what's happening here, do you? This Rebecca Lake person could take over the eighth grade. Tie up every guy. Just wipe us right off the map. POW! That's it! We're gone. I, for one, am not going to let that happen."

"You make it sound like we can kick her out school," Mona giggled.

"Or worse!" Robin exclaimed. "Bury her alive somewhere!"

"This isn't funny," Alexa replied calmly. "The way I see it, we've got an important choice here. Ever hear the expression 'If you can't beat 'em, join 'em'? "

"Sure," Mona replied. "But, really. Does this have to be such a dramatic decision? I mean, we don't even know her. She could be a terrible person. She could have a miserable personality, and all of this worrying could be for nothing. . . . "

"She's just as lively as can be," Alexa replied curtly. "Trust me. She's just a bundle of light, bright, fun. It's nauseating."

"Alexa! So what!" Mona tried again. "You're fun, too! And Robin is talented and cute and full of energy. What difference does it . . . "

Alexa cut her off with an abrupt wave of her hand. All that was true. Even Mona possessed an awful lot of star power. In fact, she was dark and mysterious-looking herself.

She just wasn't a scene stealer. Mona preferred the background, which suited Alexa just fine.

"Look," Alexa began slowly, carefully, as if she were talking to a child. She turned around to admire the way her jeans flattered her from behind. "I know that we don't know that much about this girl. Actually, erase that. We know NOTHING about this girl. But, frankly, what does it matter? That's not the point. Keeping her on our side, however, is."

"Honestly, Alexa," Mona argued. "Isn't there a middle ground here?"

"No," Alexa snapped. "If we ignore her, or make her an enemy, she may decide to do just as she pleases. If she does, and there's some kind of all-out competition for guys or even girls, who's to say we'll win?"

"Win what?" Mona cried out. "Besides," she continued, "it may not work!" Mona giggled. "She may still steal some guys away!"

"Very funny, Mona." Alexa flashed her an annoyed glance. "No one is going to steal some guy from me. You may be used to that kind of thing, but I'm not."

Instantly Mona looked away. Alexa bit down hard on her lower lip. That was a mistake. Why did she always do that? Strike out so fast? Mona was forever petrified that Joe, her boyfriend from camp, would stop calling.

"I . . . I . . . didn't mean that, really, Mona," Alexa apologized. "You just got me mad. You know Joe is wild about you."

Mona nodded. "That's okay." She smiled softly and began braiding her long, thick, dark hair. "You're just worried about Mac. But, honestly,

14

Alexa, he's another one you hardly know. You just want to win him over on principle."

Alexa shrugged. Maybe. Maybe not. She smiled meekly at Mona. For the hundredth time, she wondered what it was Mona seemed to value so much in their friendship. If she only knew. So she could concentrate on it . . . when she had the time. It had something to do with Mona's unhappy home life and Alexa's way of making her feel that she fit in. It was sincere, too. Alexa admired her a lot.

"Well, I think we should take it slow with Rebecca," Robin suggested. "Maybe everyone will get sick of her soon."

"I say no," Alexa replied. "I think we should get real close real fast. Trust me. It's the safest thing."

"Okay. I could go along with that," Robin grinned.

Alexa turned to Mona. "If she's not worth the trouble, we can just dump her, you know."

Mona shook her head. "Not smart. I'm warning you."

Alexa smiled patiently.

"Mona, you warn me about lots of things, and most of the time everything falls into place just fine."

"It does?" Mona asked with no small amount of amusement.

Alexa closed her eyes for a moment in an effort to control herself. For an insecure person, Mona sure spoke up a lot.

"I'm planning to invite Rebecca over for a little visit," Alexa finally said stiffly. "A kind of 'get to know you' thing. Why don't both of you come, too?"

Mona sighed. "Okay, but don't expect me to be super-warm to her."

Alexa shrugged. "Leave that to me."

"I'll be nice," Robin announced. "After all, why not? Rebecca could turn out to be terrific!"

Alexa grimaced.

She certainly hoped not.

Beauty she could combat. Terrific would be an uphill battle.

3

"I love your room," Gina sighed, leaning back on a huge cotton floor pillow that was covered in an American Indian motif. She looked around Priscilla's large, colorful, airy bedroom. "It's so . . . so . . . funky."

Priscilla nodded proudly and glanced at the mural she'd just recently painted next to her bed. It was the image of a window opening onto a pristine country garden. She'd worked on the details for weeks. The oak tree especially. It made her feel good just to look at it.

It set her dreaming. About summers at the lake, about having her own art exhibit . . . about Adam Miller. She couldn't be sure, but it looked as if he had been watching her at the library today.

"Could you do something like that on one of my walls?" Margo asked cheerfully. "But could you paint it to order? You know. Richie McCormick could be standing there holding his arms out to me. Longingly." She pouted as everyone started chuckling. "So? What's wrong with that?"

"I think it's time for Priscilla to call this meeting to order," Vivienne proclaimed. "Nothing's wrong with it, Margo," she grinned. "It's just the part about the longing . . . " Suddenly Vivienne began to blush. Self-consciously, she looked away.

"It is time," Priscilla agreed. She traced her finger over the beaded front of the red sweater she'd picked up in a secondhand shop.

Reaching for her Practically Popular Crowd notebook, Priscilla's eye fell on the algebra quiz that was lying, still neatly folded, on her desk.

Why did the letter D have to be so big? So round? So red?

Couldn't she just forget about it? What did it mean, anyway?

Nothing. That's what.

Her eyes rested on Michelle and Margo, just a pinch of anxiety nibbling at her certainty. Well, she had it all figured out. She'd be very casual at this meeting. Mention her failing algebra grade, bring up the science quiz, and then wait for everyone to tell her she's very smart. Next — and this was key — she'd sign them all up for a little more informal tutoring.

Things were bound to improve.

Priscilla smiled. Yes. She had it together. Just the way she liked it.

"I declare this meeting of the eighth-grade Practically Popular Crowd in session, and . . . " — Priscilla took a deep breath as she opened her notebook to take notes — "I have something to say," she added sheepishly.

"Me, too!" Vivienne called out excitedly.

"Priscilla first," Michelle interjected. "It's her room."

"Well . . . " Priscilla looked around at her friends with a faint smile on her lips. "You know me. Art, art, art. I kind of blew the algebra test, and the science quiz messed me up. So . . . "

Priscilla leaned back against the wall with a soft sigh. This was the good part. This was where everyone said nice, supportive things. Things they really believed.

Things that, Priscilla was beginning to worry, just a little bit, weren't completely true.

There was a beat of silence.

"You know, Priscilla, we've been trying to help you," Gina said gently. "If it isn't working, maybe you should talk to the teacher about some real tutoring."

Priscilla blinked her eyes a few times, as if she were trying to wake up from a bad dream. "Excuse me?"

"Well, Pris," Michelle began carefully. "You've been having some trouble, and maybe we're not good enough teachers to . . . "

Priscilla could feel her stomach tightening.

This was unreal. Ridiculous. What were her friends saying exactly? That she needed serious help? The kind stupid people needed? Is that what they thought of her? She looked from girl to girl. Her friends? Her confidantes? Her equals? Supposedly . . .

Priscilla set her lips together in a grim line. Abruptly she stood up, walked across the room, and picked up a sketch pencil. Returning to her spot, she sat down and smiled around the room.

Never again. She'd never mention school or grades again. She'd make them think everything was fine. It was just too humiliating to take. She didn't need that kind of help. Not her.

"Well, look," she offered philosophically as she began nervously sketching a tree, thick with leaves, on the open notebook page, "I'll get it together. I always do." Holding her back straight and her head high, she looked from girl to girl. "You know me," she said with a broad confident grin.

"Gina's probably right about the tutoring thing," Margo persisted gently. "It would help a lot, I'm sure. Hasn't the teacher said anything to you?"

Priscilla shrugged. Actually, she had. She had asked Priscilla to come for a meeting Friday afternoon. Priscilla was dreading it.

"Of course not," Priscilla laughed. She shook her head with mock confusion. "I don't blow every test. And my homework is great!" Her pencil was flying now across the page. The tree looked as if it were being blown in a mighty storm. "Let's change the subject." She looked up and smiled broadly.

"Good! I have something VERY important to discuss," Vivienne announced. She scrambled to her feet and started pacing about the room. "You guys know how much I love this crowd. Right?"

Everyone nodded.

"And that I think we're just about a perfect unit?"

Again everyone nodded enthusiastically. Pridefully.

Priscilla cocked her head to one side and studied Vivienne carefully. What exactly did she mean by "just about"?

Vivienne took a deep breath. "And I suppose you would all agree that if we are to grow together, we have to accept change. Maybe even encourage it."

For a long moment everyone was silent.

"Well, like what kind of change?" Gina asked softly.

"Changes in ourselves, changes in our lives, that kind of thing," Vivienne answered. She coughed nervously.

"Get to the point, Ms. Bennis," Margo snipped good-naturedly. "You sound like a politician. You're talking a lot, but you're not saying much."

"Okay, okay," Vivienne responded, holding up both hands. "Here it is. The change I'm talking about is Rebecca Lake."

"What about her?" Michelle asked. "Has she changed? And if she has, how would you know? We just met her!"

"I want to invite her into The Practically Popular Crowd," Viv blurted out. "*Voilà!* There it is. That's what I want."

"You're kidding!" Priscilla practically choked. "We just met her! I'm not even sure I like her!"

"She's great," Vivienne replied matter-of-factly. "She's just what we need, too."

"What? What do we need?" Michelle asked incredulously. "I don't feel like we need a thing."

"Glamour," Vivienne replied. "Alexa Craft glamour, only without the garbage." Almost shyly she looked around the room from girl to girl. "Has anyone noticed the mascara I'm wearing? Rebecca picked the color out for me. I think it looks very natural. She says so, too. Don't you?"

Michelle shook her head. "Boy, and you get on me for always being jealous of Alexa."

"You know, actually Rebecca is very nice," Gina commented. "And I think she's lonely."

"Exactly!" Vivienne jumped in.

"And she probably would be a nice addition," Margo added. "Just yesterday she helped me smooth out that frizzy part of my hair that drives me so crazy, and she was very enthusiastic about joining some class committees." Margo held her chin up proudly. "She said she wished she were as committed a person as I am."

Priscilla peered around her room in disbelief. Had everyone gone out of their minds? How could one girl have brainwashed so many people in so short a time?

"Well, I for one, don't like it," she said firmly. "And I think you guys are moving too fast." She folded her arms across her chest. They'd listen to her. They always did when it came to major decisions.

"I thought you'd say that," Vivienne responded coolly.

"Oh, yes?" Priscilla asked, her stomach beginning to tighten once more. "Why?"

"Because," Vivienne paused for effect, "Rebecca is as good an artist as you are."

For a long moment there was nothing but silence in the room.

Priscilla turned to stare at the mural, willing herself to fly into the country garden, onto the little stone bridge. Where she could sit, contentedly, for the rest of this stupid meeting.

"Stop it, Viv," Michelle's voice suddenly cut through the air. "Just because you think Rebecca would be nice to have in our crowd doesn't mean Priscilla has to agree. We hardly know Rebecca!" She shook her head. "You have got to stop jumping on people."

Vivienne nodded sheepishly. "I know that," she mumbled. Her eyes returned to Priscilla. "Okay. I'm listening. Why don't you like the idea?"

Priscilla turned away from Vivienne. "I don't know what the reason really is. I . . . I . . . don't trust her." She closed her eyes for a moment. Vivienne with her awesome brain was suddenly making her very nervous. Distrustful of even herself. It was a horrible feeling. Was it possible that Vivienne was right? That she disliked Rebecca Lake because she was the talented R.L.?

A few seconds of silence went by.

"Well, so far I haven't heard any real arguments against Rebecca," Vivienne observed, brightening considerably. "So, why don't we all just think about it?" She turned toward Priscilla. "Honestly, though, if I were you, I wouldn't judge people so fast."

Priscilla's head shot back as if she'd been slapped. Vivienne had gone too far. The words came flying out of her mouth before she even knew what she was about to say. "Look who's talking!" she almost started to laugh. "Rebecca compliments you, pays you lots of attention, and suddenly you think she's the best thing in the world! Don't you see this is about you getting back at

Alexa for having dumped you? You want to prove you can be friends with someone hot like her!"

Priscilla looked around the room, anticipating support.

She'd spoken the truth. Made sense. The Crowd would see that. "The Alexa Trio isn't worth the effort," she added emphatically.

For a moment no one said a word.

"I cannot believe you just said that," Vivienne finally spoke, with icy directness. "Or maybe you just happened to notice the big fat one hundred percent on Rebecca's algebra homework today. I had to help her just a little bit and POW! She got it!"

Instantly, feeling like a deflated balloon, Priscilla bowed her head. Had she seen the one hundred percent? Was that why she was so against her? She didn't remember seeing it, but who knew?

She clutched her pencil tightly. What was happening to her? She used to know just what she thought, and why, too. . . .

"Actually, Viv," Margo chimed in, "you did a little more than help Rebecca. You worked out two of the problems for her."

"No," Vivienne insisted defensively. "She was just a little confused, so I did them WITH her. That's a big difference."

"Whatever. Look, Viv, we'll think about it," Michelle declared. "We'll think about whether or not to include Rebecca, and decide soon. Is that acceptable to everyone?"

"Sure. But let's make it real soon," Vivienne proposed. She nodded encouragingly at everyone. "I'm excited." She glanced at Priscilla uneasily. "I didn't mean all that. I'm just feeling, I don't know . . . all worked up."

Priscilla shrugged. Actually, she knew precisely how Vivienne felt.

"Pris, aren't you supposed to be taking notes?" Gina asked softly.

Priscilla looked down at her pad and, with an angry flourish, added a few bolts of lightning to her sketch.

Then she picked up a pen and, holding it up for all to see, turned to the next blank page in her book and wrote: TODAY WE DISCUSSED ADMITTING A NEW MEMBER TO THE PRACTICALLY POPULAR CROWD. HER NAME IS REBECCCA LAKE. WE DON'T KNOW HER. I DON'T LIKE HER. BUT WE HAVE TO DECIDE SOON. FOR NO REASON.

Priscilla paused to glance at Vivienne. IT MAKES NO SENSE, she added to the page. BUT, THEN, THESE DAYS, WHAT EXACTLY DO I KNOW?

4

"**A**nd this," Alexa motioned proudly toward the dining room Thursday afternoon, "is the formal eating area." She walked over and ran her fingers lightly over the rich mahogany table. "My father had this specially made. . . . " She turned and gazed at Rebecca.

To check for approval. An impressed smile. Just a touch of envy.

Rebecca's eyes were traveling about the peach-and-celadon room, her mouth slightly open.

It appeared things were going beautifully.

"Your house is just gorgeous," Rebecca breathed.

"It is," Robin interjected with an exaggerated nod. She nudged Mona, who managed an insincere smile.

"Thank you," Alexa replied, aiming for a modest tone. "Let's go to the kitchen now. We can all have a diet snack and just kind of get to know each other. Okay?" Without waiting for an answer, Alexa started walking briskly toward the kitchen doors. Of course it was okay. She was running the show. And the name of the show was "Snag Rebecca Before Anyone Else Does."

"Mimi!" Alexa called out cheerfully to the Crafts' Jamaican housekeeper. "Meet our new friend, Rebecca Lake! Rebecca, this is Mimi. She . . . " It was hard to describe Mimi's role in the family. Housekeeper, friend, Alexa's special confidante, cook . . . the list was endless. "She works for my family," Alexa finally finished.

For a moment she wondered if the word "maid" would have sounded better. More upper crust and everything. Rebecca looked like she had ten maids. Of course Alexa couldn't have used the word anyway. Mimi hated it.

"Hello," Rebecca said with obvious disinterest, barely nodding in Mimi's direction. "What a gorgeous kitchen, too!" She turned to Alexa. "How about those low-cal things?" She gazed from girl to girl. "I'd love my figure to be as good as all of yours!" She ran her hands over her perfectly flat stomach as if it needed to be slimmer still.

Alexa looked down, self-consciously, at her own stomach. Whose was flatter? It was hard to tell.

"Well, there's those no-good, skinny cookies in that cabinet over the toaster," Mimi suggested with what Alexa could tell was a forced brightness. "Those'll keep you gals goin'."

Rebecca again barely nodded in Mimi's direction and then turned expectantly to Alexa.

Glancing nervously at Mimi's stony expression, Alexa started talking quickly. "Let's just take those cookies up to my room, girls, okay?" Mimi didn't like rude people. Alexa grabbed the cookie bag from the cabinet and sped through the kitchen doors.

"Practicing for a marathon?" Mona called out from behind as she watched the three girls race up the circular staircase. "What's the rush?"

Shooting her an annoyed look, Alexa flew down the hall, threw open the door of her room, and collapsed on her bed. "Finally!" she cried out with a smile. "Privacy!"

Rebecca grinned. "Oh, I feel so great with you guys. So lucky," she gushed.

Alexa nodded. Of course she did. Popular people were, well, electric.

"So, tell us about you. How come your family moved?" Alexa asked, leaning back against her bedroom wall. "I heard something about Michigan?"

Rebecca smiled. "My father started a public relations business there, and we're here to open up a New York area office. He's brilliant and fabulous and cool. I'm going to be seeing his new office soon. He's very busy." She rubbed her hands together. "But that's okay. It gives me lots of free time."

"That's great," Robin chimed in. "My mother is always around. She works out of our house part-time. She's a freelance copywriter." She shrugged. "What about your mother?"

"Oh, but your mom helps children," Rebecca argued, ignoring the question. "She must be a terrific person."

Robin grinned from ear to ear. "Yes." She squared her shoulders. "I suppose she is. And yours?"

"What about you, Mona?" Rebecca asked sweetly, ignoring the question yet again. "What should I know about you?"

Mona shrugged and shot Alexa a warning look. "Nothing. I'm not much of a talker, really. Not at first, anyway."

Rebecca nodded. "That's okay. You seem like a very interesting person, though. Very smart."

Alexa cleared her throat and looked away. This wasn't going the way she'd intended. She was supposed to be the lead player here. The center of attention. The one whom Rebecca was close to. Attached to.

And thus unwilling to double-cross. In any way.

"You know," Alexa blurted out. "It was my idea to have you over. To kind of bring you into the group." She smiled. "I actually thought you seemed very . . . special."

Flattery. What a disgusting, phony business. She couldn't remember the last time she'd actually used it to win a girl over. Sure, she flattered boys regularly. But that was, well, natural. Alexa glanced down at her chest. Not that they ever listened. They were too busy looking.

A glimmer of pleasure flashed across Rebecca's face. "And I'm so glad you did invite me," she gushed once more. "You can't know. Especially, well, never mind . . . "

"No," Alexa giggled. "Tell us. Especially what?"

Something was about to get interesting. Gossipy. She could feel it.

"Well, I really shouldn't say," Rebecca smiled sweetly.

"Okay. Then, well, don't," Mona responded matter-of-factly.

"Oh, don't be ridiculous." Alexa waved Mona's words away with her hand. "We're friends here. Especially what?"

"Well, actually" — Rebecca leaned in slightly as if she were telling a secret — "I've sort of been wondering about these girls who keep buzzing around me a lot. . . . "

Alexa grinned broadly. What a piece of cake. And she thought those Practically Great Girls, or whatever, were competition. "Yes, well, what about them?"

Rebecca shrugged. "I certainly think they're nice enough. I do. Believe me. Vivienne is so earnest and all. But, well" — she looked from Alexa to Mona to Robin and then back at Alexa — "they aren't exactly like you guys."

"What do you mean?" Robin giggled, reaching into her bag and pulling out some blush. "Tell us . . . "

Rebecca giggled. "Oh, Robin. Look in the mirror. What do you think I mean?" She turned to Alexa. "Certainly, you must know . . . "

Alexa nodded knowingly. Actually, Rebecca wasn't half-bad. She was perceptive. She was strong. She was sure of herself. Typically those traits in other people made Alexa feel nervous. Insecure. But not this time. No. She was playing this right. Rebecca was going to be a friend.

What fun.

"Sure I do. But you know" — Alexa began picking at the embroidered lavender flowers on her bedspread — "it takes all kinds."

Actually, she and Alexa might do well as a team.

A kind of one, two punch.

"Of course," Rebecca agreed quickly. "I mean, don't get me wrong. I like them. It's just that . . . "

"Well, don't get me wrong," Alexa smirked. "I don't. I used to like them. But to tell you the truth, I got a little bored with every last one of them after a while, and now, well, we have some kind of, I don't know, ongoing feud." She giggled again. "Of course, I don't know why. Generally, I leave them alone."

"Excuse me?" Mona chimed in. "You do what?"

"I said I leave them alone," Alexa replied obstinately. "Most of the time. Unless they mess with me, and then I get, well . . . "

"Ugly," Mona finished for her with a big smile. Then, noticing Alexa's frigid stare, she backed down. "But they deserve it. Kind of." She made a face at Alexa.

"Well," Rebecca stood up. "I'm sure glad you guys are interested in me. Which reminds me . . . " She threw open Alexa's closet door and gave herself a once-over in the mirror. She straightened her hot-pink Lycra skirt. "Who ARE the hot guys?"

"Huh?" Robin asked. "What do you mean?"

Rebecca wiggled her hips. "You know. The cool guys."

Alexa flipped her thick blonde hair over her shoulders. Okay. This was where she could prove her stuff. Win Rebecca over. Keep her on her side. Forever and a day.

Popping off of her bed, she reached into her desk drawer and pulled out a picture of Mac Todd. Her latest target. It was only a matter of time till she landed him.

"Well, this one is mine, but we can find you more of these if that's what you're looking for," Alexa grinned proudly.

Rebecca took the picture and studied it for a few seconds. "Yes! Yes! This is what I had in

33

mind," she laughed. She tossed her own thick, dark brown hair behind her shoulders. "I think he would do just fine . . . I . . . I . . . mean some-one just like him, of course!"

"Of course," Alexa said quickly. Deliberately. That was quite a slip. It probably meant nothing. Still.

"He and I are becoming a thing," Alexa said gently. Seriously. "So of course you realize . . . "

"Sure, sure," Rebecca giggled, holding both hands up. "He's off-limits. But if he has a friend . . . "

Alexa nodded. "Sure. And if he doesn't have one at Port Andrews High, he may have one in the next town."

"Good!" Rebecca tittered. "Not that I'm completely boy-crazy, but you know . . . "

"Sure we do," Robin nodded enthusiastically.

Rebecca looked down at her watch. "Uh-oh! I've got to go. I'm meeting my dad. Maybe we can do this again. Okay?" She picked up her cranberry leather shoulder bag and headed for the door.

"I'll walk you out," Alexa insisted, following her into the hallway and down the stairs. Reaching the front door, Alexa opened it for Rebecca and smiled broadly. "Maybe you can meet us tomorrow. In the park. It's a great place to watch guys."

"Call me," Rebecca nodded. "Sounds good."
And with that, the most glamourous girl Alexa

could remember seeing in Port Andrews, other than herself, walked out the door.

"I don't like that one," Mimi's voice cut through the air.

Alexa whirled around to see Mimi walking through the swinging doors leading from the kitchen.

"How can you say that? You don't know her."

"Neither do you," Mimi replied coolly, leaning against the wall.

"Well, that's not exactly true," Alexa insisted.

"Well, then, what you know you don't want to know," Mimi continued matter-of-factly. "And it's going to come up from behind and give you a good pinch." She nodded toward the door. "That girl's like a dark, shiny, invitin' pool of water on a hot day. It's real temptin' till you dive in and find out it's full of jellyfish."

"You're just saying that because she ignored you," Alexa insisted defensively.

Mimi shrugged and smiled. "You think I care 'bout that? You got that wrong. I care 'bout you."

"Well, think whatever you want." Alexa tried to smile as if she were completely unperturbed. Which wasn't so. The entire Craft family knew that Mimi Summers was a terrific judge of character.

Alexa started back upstairs. "I'm going to get beautiful."

"Try gettin' smart, too," Mimi called out. "You're gonna need all those brains you keep tuckin' away to deal with that one, let me tell you. . . . "

Alexa paused as she reached the second-floor landing.

Rebecca was fine. Just a little, well, conceited. A little overly gushy. Probably not the most trustworthy girl in the world.

But, then, neither was Alexa.

And, anyway, Rebecca needed her. Which was the perfect place to be, with a girl like that.

She smiled. Really, they were so much alike.

Equals, in fact.

It made for a perfect relationship.

Unless, of course, one of them got more equal than the other.

5

Priscilla stood nervously outside of Mrs. Simon's classroom and checked her watch. She was early. No need to rush this talk. She slipped to the floor and, sitting with her back against the light green wall, pulled out her elementary algebra text.

She flipped to the first chapter.

There they were again. All those X's. All those unknowns. All those questions. Honestly. Who cared?

Glancing absentmindedly to her right, Priscilla suddenly became aware of a pair of beat-up white sneakers standing a few feet away. Slowly her eyes traveled up the blue-jeaned legs and familiar red-and-blue-striped jersey to find Adam Miller gazing uncertainly in her direction. He swept back a lock of straight blond hair with his free hand.

Priscilla smiled brightly. "Hi," she said. Not too

excitedly, but as invitingly as she could manage. She didn't want to come on strong. Scare him off. He just seemed so . . . reserved.

Adam smiled, took an obvious deep breath, and began walking toward her, talking all the way as if he were a wound-up mechanical doll. "I noticed there's a new art exhibit at the River Gallery in town, and I thought on Saturday you might like to go and see it. I know you enjoy art and . . . "

Priscilla began nodding before he could finish. Unbelievable! She was right. He had been watching her. Maybe even admiring her. She could feel a pleasurable tingle travel through her body. "I'd love to." She smiled at him encouragingly. "I really would."

Suddenly the door behind her swung open, and Mrs. Simon was standing right beside her. "Priscilla," she said warmly, "come in. Please."

Collecting her books, Priscilla scurried to her feet. She could feel her face turning red. What if Adam suspected the reason she was here? She'd rather die. Quickly, Priscilla turned toward him and whispered, "I was out sick. I missed some notes." Adam smiled knowingly. Priscilla grinned back confidently and then turned to follow Mrs. Simon into the classroom. He'd bought it. She could tell.

Mrs. Simon motioned to a chair she'd pulled up next to the side of her desk. Priscilla settled in it, placing her algebra book on top. To prove she'd been studying. To prove she cared. To prove things would change.

Priscilla crossed her ankles. Relax, she instructed herself. This is probably nothing.

"Priscilla, first of all, I want you to know I think you are a very bright girl. . . . "

Priscilla smiled. Okay. This wasn't so bad. Here was a good teacher. And she was telling Priscilla she was absolutely smart. She'd worried for nothing.

Priscilla nodded with relief.

"But I notice you're having some trouble in my class."

"I know I am," Priscilla chimed in quickly. "But that will change. I've been a little preoccupied. But I'm going to study harder now." There, that sounded strong. Convincing.

Mrs. Simon nodded. "Glad to hear that."

Priscilla leaned back in her chair. Thank goodness. This talk was almost over. She'd be out of here in a minute.

"And I don't want you to regard what I'm about to say as a punishment. . . . "

Priscilla stared at Mrs. Simon blankly. What in heaven's name was she talking about?

"I feel it's important for you to go into the math section that moves at a slightly more measured pace."

"Wh-what do you mean?" Priscilla stammered. She began twirling a piece of hair nervously between two fingers. Mrs. Simon meant something big. She could feel it.

"I'm saying that I think you should try Ms. Williams' class."

For a moment, Priscilla sat in stunned silence. She hadn't heard right. That was all. She cleared her throat, waiting for Mrs. Simon to clarify. To expand. To add "just for a day," or "if you'd like . . . "

But she didn't. She was quiet. Very still.

Priscilla lowered her eyes. "You mean the stupid class . . . " she answered in a muffled voice, as if the words were a string of curses. She could feel her heart beginning to beat very hard. She placed both hands on Mrs. Simon's desk. "I . . . I . . . don't need that. I thought you just said I'm smart. . . . "

Mrs. Simon smiled kindly. "Priscilla, you are smart. You're creative. You're an interesting girl. But no one can be strong in everything. It appears that you have some trouble understanding many basic algebraic principles, and . . . "

"That's not true," Priscilla whispered, tears now filling her eyes. "I just need a little more time. . . . "

"No, Priscilla," Mrs. Simon said firmly. "Your grades have been consistently poor. What you need is a class in which you can do some catching up. A class that moves more slowly . . . "

"But what will I tell my friends?" Priscilla implored. "They're going to think I'm stupid! None of them have to move classes!"

"You'll tell them this is what you need right now," she offered, not unkindly.

Priscilla looked down at her lap. What she needed right now was not the point.

Maybe it should have been. But it wasn't.

"Besides, it's a terrific class. They cover the same material, but a little differently," Mrs. Simon interrupted her thoughts. "And, Priscilla, many of the students are very bright. Their strengths just lie elsewhere."

"I don't want to do it," Priscilla said quietly. She studied Mrs. Simon tentatively. "What if I say no?"

Mrs. Simon covered Priscilla's hand with her own. "Won't you feel better, understanding the work? What difference does it make which class you're in, if you have a better chance to learn?"

Priscilla shook her head. "You don't understand . . . "

"But I do." Mrs. Simon shook her head. "Eighth grade is very different from seventh. Lots of kids are having adjustment problems. You'll catch on. People do. . . . "

Abruptly Priscilla stood up. She had to get away. First her friends, now this. What was next? The possibilities filled her with horror. The slow

English section? History for dummies? "When do I start the new class?" Priscilla asked as she moved away from her chair.

"Tuesday," Mrs. Simon smiled brightly. "Ms. Williams' section doesn't meet on Monday."

Priscilla nodded, turned, and walked toward the door. "Thanks," she murmured softly over her shoulder.

Visions of The Practically Popular Crowd flashed before her eyes. She had to tell them. There was no avoiding it. What ever would they think? Conclude? That she couldn't keep up? That she wasn't Practically Popular material anymore?

Priscilla's hand flew to her mouth. As if to cover it. To keep it from saying anything. To anyone.

She stood perfectly still in the hallway for a long moment.

Then she turned and began walking purposefully down the hall, toward the one place she still, absolutely, belonged.

Priscilla studied the pastels before her.

Maybe a seascape with crashing waves.

Or a lightning-filled sky over a lone farmhouse.

Or maybe the art class assignment. A self-portrait.

Priscilla frowned. She wasn't that good at faces. And right now, she didn't much feel like studying her own.

Silently she picked up a rich gray pastel and began to work on a stormy sky. Seconds later she selected a softer gray for contrast, and then a stark white. For depth. For accent.

She could feel herself growing more peaceful. She could lose herself in this. Always. She could hear the thunder overhead. She could almost feel the dampness. She stepped back.

Perhaps a bird. A sea gull, just below the clouds . . .

"Nice . . . " a familiar voice said from somewhere behind her.

Priscilla whipped around with surprise.

Adam Miller stood off to the side, studying the piece. "Nice mood," he said. He smiled at her self-consciously. "I'm not following you. I was researching something in the library."

Priscilla nodded stiffly and then looked away quickly. Adam Miller.

What, in the end, would he want with her?

She picked up a deep-blue pastel. He was out of her league.

She shouldn't have agreed to go out with him. Her eyes began to well up. He'd realize she wasn't smart enough in no time flat.

Priscilla looked back at her work, then placed the pastel down. The mood was broken.

"Please, go on," Adam said, stepping backwards. "I didn't mean to disturb you. I'm sorry. I was just walking by. . . . "

"It's okay," Priscilla mumbled. "Really, I was running out of time anyway. This was just a spur-of-the-moment thing."

"There you are!" Margo called out gaily as she bounded into the art room. Spotting Adam, she began pulling at her oversized top to make sure it stayed down. Covered everything. "We've been waiting for you!"

Priscilla mustered a bright smile and shrugged. "I was working on something." She picked up a slightly soiled rag and wiped off her hands. She could see, out of the corner of her eye, Adam edging very slowly toward the door.

"Bye," she called out dully.

He nodded and then disappeared through the door.

Priscilla sighed. He'd probably never ask another girl out his whole life.

"So, should we all go to The Corner Shop and get a soda or something?" Margo suggested as the other members of The Practically Popular Crowd filed into the room.

"Good idea," Michelle nodded. "I haven't been talking about it much, but I have that little flute recital coming up on Monday. I'm real nervous. Maybe just hanging out will calm me down. . . . "

Priscilla looked around at her four closest, smart friends.

Was it actually possible she wasn't right for them anymore? Was it possible she no longer fit in?

Priscilla began chewing on the inside of her mouth. If only she didn't have to tell them about Ms. Williams' class. She could feel the tears threatening to fall once more.

"Oh, look!" Vivienne suddenly called out, "Rebecca just walked by." Instantly she raced to the doorway. "Rebecca!" she called out excitedly. A moment later she disappeared.

Priscilla cringed. Something about it was so . . . sickening.

She stepped way from the easel to rinse off her hands.

"Hello, everyone," Rebecca bounced into the room moments later, Viv close behind. She waved happily. "A soda sounds great!" She looked at Viv. "And so does some help with my science homework. Boy, it's hard catching up. . . . " She grinned. "Alexa offered to help, but she's not as smart as all of you."

"How true," Vivienne waved it away. "You don't need her."

"Are you having trouble?" Gina asked. "We could all give you some help. It must be hard changing schools."

Priscilla stared up at the ceiling, filled with resentment.

So that's how everyone was thinking. Rebecca, they could help. She, however, was just a little too dumb.

A little too beyond their assistance.

"That would be great," Rebecca smiled warmly. She picked up a sketch pencil, blithely removed the piece Priscilla had been working on, and clipped fresh paper to the easel.

Priscilla looked on, stunned. There were other, already empty, easels she could have used.

Rebecca picked up a pastel. "How 'bout that portrait assignment?" She smiled at Priscilla.

Priscilla nodded numbly, still in shock. Of course, she *had* stepped away from the easel. Maybe Rebecca didn't realize it was her work. But, then again, whose would it have been?

Rebecca continued chattering. "I love working on portraits. . . . " Again she turned to Priscilla. "Don't you?"

Priscilla shrugged. Faces were difficult for her. She looked at Rebecca thoughtfully. Had she seen Priscilla's portrait work in progress? She'd left it out by mistake on an easel yesterday. Is that why Rebecca had brought it up? To embarrass her?

Priscilla looked down at the linoleum floor with a frown. Was it her imagination, or was Rebecca Lake trying to put her down?

"Oh, Priscilla's always complaining about faces!" Margo giggled. "She does great profiles, though."

Rebecca nodded and began working away. The girls gathered around. In minutes, a face that resembled Priscilla's began to appear.

"Actually, at home, for practice, I was working on a portrait of you, Margo," Rebecca commented sweetly. "Hope you don't mind."

"MIND!" Margo answered excitedly. "REALLY? How neat!"

"Oh! Could you do one of all of us?" Viv asked. She flashed Rebecca a big smile. "We'd love it. It would be like a special Crowd thing. . . . "

Instantly Priscilla turned away from the easel. She took a deep, shaky breath and let it out very slowly. Her eyes fell on a jumble of paintbrushes in a large metal box. She began to straighten them out.

A special Crowd thing?

Art by Rebecca Lake?

But that was her territory. Her gift. Her specialness.

Priscilla removed a pencil from the box and replaced it with a slim delicate brush that was resting on the tabletop.

She shuddered slightly and lowered her head to hide the tears.

Poor pencil.

She knew just how it felt.

6

Alexa smiled invitingly and leaned across the table, allowing her thick blonde hair to fall semicarelessly over one eye.

Her most sexy look. She glanced down for a second. The deep scooped-neck navy sweater didn't hurt, either.

"I was wondering when we'd run into each other again," she purred. Low and with just the right touch of promise of things to come.

Mac grinned appreciatively, running a hand through his short, curly, light brown hair. "Me, too. That Saturday afternoon was great. You're some tennis player."

Alexa nodded and allowed her eyes to travel over Mac's broad shoulders. And he was some kisser. What a hunk. She smiled into his sparkly deep brown eyes. Ninth grade sure had some handsome guys.

"Hi, Mac!" a tall, slim, dark-haired girl called

out as she burst through the door of Leo's, heading straight for the counter.

Alexa frowned. Ninth-grade girls were a drag. And what was it these days with pretty, dark-haired people?

"Don't worry, Alexa," Mac laughed. "I'm not meeting her here."

Alexa shot him a stinging look. Careful, a voice inside her head whispered. Temper.

"Why would I worry?" she asked him icily. Instantly she softened her expression. "Mac," she paused for effect, "if you like me, you're going to like me, no matter who's around." Then she smiled softly. With maturity. And confidence.

And hidden annoyance.

Mac was great. She wanted to date him. But if there was one thing she hated, it was cocky guys. The ones who thought they knew her. Could read her. The ones who thought they had her all wrapped up.

The ones who were right.

"So how's school going?" Mac asked casually as he took a bite out of his pepperoni pizza. "Eighth grade was a real shocker for me. Took me half a year to get into the swing of things."

Alexa hesitated. This was exactly the kind of moment that confused her. What did boys want to hear, anyway? The truth? She was doing fine? Maybe he wouldn't like that she was finding eighth grade all right when he hadn't. On the other hand, he was a smart guy. Wouldn't he appreciate knowing Alexa was keeping up?

It was a tough call.

"I'm doing okay," Alexa shrugged. "Not too bad in some things, and not so well in others." There, that was brilliant. Actually, she smiled to herself, she was probably smarter than she thought.

"I'm thinking about looking for a new racquet next week. Wednesday afternoon. Do you want to come?" Mac asked casually. "You'd probably be a big help."

Alexa tossed her hair back over her shoulders. "Oh, I believe that could be arranged," she laughed. "And, then, maybe afterwards you could come back to my house for something to eat?"

Instantly Alexa looked away. She'd never liked doing that sort of thing. Putting herself on the line. Asking for dates . . . even though this was technically just an add-on. But things were moving terribly slowly with Mac. He just didn't seem in much of a hurry to make anything happen between them.

A Saturday afternoon date here. A quick soda there. Which wouldn't be so bad except the invitations were two weeks apart.

What did he think? She was going to be available forever?

She could tell he liked her. He smiled at her a

lot. They'd already kissed a few times. And he was very complimentary.

So what was the problem?

Didn't he want a girlfriend?

"Alexa!" an excited familiar voice rang through the air.

Alexa looked up to find Rebecca Lake walking quickly toward their table. Ever so slightly, but enough to see, Alexa shook her head, as if to say, "No. Not now. Go away." But Rebecca kept coming. Like a steamroller.

Alexa sighed. Maybe she'd been too subtle.

"You must be Mac," Rebecca announced, much to Alexa's horror, as she stood to the side of the table. Wearing a skintight black suede skirt and a V-necked black leotard underneath, she leaned in, fetchingly, toward Mac.

"Why, yes I am," Mac replied, his eyes, Alexa noticed, moving nonstop in an effort to drink every detail of Rebecca in. "How did you know?"

Rebecca smiled and patted Alexa on the head. "She showed me your picture."

Alexa could not believe her ears. Rebecca had to be kidding. It was like a bad dream. How dare she say something so embarrassing! And right in front of her!

"A-actually," Alexa found herself stuttering, "I was showing her lots of pictures. You know, from that day at school when everyone met in the field. . . . " She turned and shot Rebecca a dark look. "Right?"

Rebecca hesitated. Then an extremely bright smile lit up her face. "Yes. I do remember. There were other people, too."

Alexa sighed with relief. Well, maybe Rebecca wasn't thinking.

"But your picture stood out, Mac," Rebecca continued, her voice slightly lower now.

Alexa stared at Rebecca in disbelief. It was just too much. What was she doing? Trying to steal her boyfriend right in front of her? Was she nuts?

"Would you like to join us?" Mac asked, speedily throwing his knapsack to the floor so that Rebecca could slide in next to him.

"I think she's kind of in a rush, aren't you?" Alexa asked bluntly. She stared at Rebecca with a studied blank expression.

Rebecca hesitated. "Not really."

"Great," Mac grinned.

"How nice," Alexa added. She watched as Rebecca's hair glistened in the light.

If only she had a tomahawk. She felt like scalping her.

"I hope I'm not interrupting anything," Rebecca began, innocent and wide-eyed. "You two look very cozy." She smiled at Alexa encouragingly. "The perfect couple."

Alexa nodded slightly and then furrowed her brow. It was like being on a roller coaster. Up and down. Fast and slow. Right side up, up side down.

What was Rebecca doing? Why didn't she just go away? At least on a roller coaster a person asked for the ride.

"Alexa and I have an understanding," Mac winked at Alexa. "Don't we?"

"Sure," Alexa smiled back knowingly. Although she had no idea what he was talking about. What was the understanding? That they were dating a little, not a lot? That they should see other people? In the best case, that he adored her but he simply had his ways? In the worst case, he liked her all right, but wanted to date whomever he pleased, including her friends?

"Sounds mysterious," Rebecca smiled. "Gee, I'd love a Coke."

"I'll get you one," Mac volunteered immediately. He looked toward the counter. "Hey, Pete! How 'bout a Coke over here, please?"

Alexa eyed him suspiciously. What was his problem? Rebecca couldn't have done that herself? She needed his voice? She had a mouth.

A real big one, in fact.

"Thank you," Rebecca murmured, tilting her head slightly to smile at Mac. "Are there more of you anywhere?"

"What do you mean?" Mac asked with a broad smile, clearly knowing precisely what she meant. He began to roll up his sleeves. Alexa looked

53

away. He was showing off. He had muscles. Big deal.

"You know, other guys who look like you, talk like you, act like you," Rebecca giggled. "Don't make me say any more."

"Yes, please don't," Alexa chimed in sarcastically. "She's blushing so . . . "

Rebecca glanced at Alexa with surprise. For a moment, everyone at the table was silent, and then suddenly, as if the role she was playing had changed, as if a new movie was now on the reel, Rebecca grew serious. "Mac, I'm just teasing you. But I would like to meet guys. Maybe you and Alexa could introduce me?"

Mac promptly nodded. Alexa wasn't sure, but he looked slightly disappointed. "I'll do my best. . . . "

Suddenly he looked up at the clock. "You know, girls, actually I've got to run. I'm supposed to be at my friend Sam's house in five minutes." Reaching across the table, he squeezed Alexa's hand. "I'll call you."

He smiled at Rebecca. "I'll be in touch. Good to meet you." And with that, he slid out the side of the booth, picked up his knapsack, and walked over to the cashier.

Instantly Rebecca leaned across the table. "How did I do?"

Alexa almost choked. "H-h-how did you do?" she repeated in disbelief. It was incredible. The question was crazy. What did she mean — was she a good boyfriend-stealer?

"Do you think I impressed him?" Rebecca continued, her eyes as wide as she could make them. "Maybe he'll set me up?" She grinned. "I wanted to show him my style."

Alexa leaned back in the booth. Was it possible? Was that all this was? Rebecca's crazy attempt to make sure Mac introduced her to his friends? She wasn't actually flirting with Mac? She was just showing him how she would flirt if he *was* one of his friends?

Alexa hesitated. What a method. It was so outrageous, it was almost believable.

Which made Alexa very nervous. That was exactly how *she* worked. She kept everybody guessing. What was real, what wasn't? Very few people ever knew.

A person had to be very alert.

"Listen, Rebecca. What's up?" Alexa asked bluntly. "I mean, it looked to me like you were coming on to Mac plain and simple."

Rebecca leaned back as if she'd been slapped.

"Alexa! I would never do that. What do I seem like to you? Stupid? Besides, that would be terrible of me!"

Alexa nodded, relaxing a little. That sounded real enough. "Well, look, next time you can probably be charming without acting so . . . so . . . well, you know." She smiled. Thank goodness.

Rebecca was some operator. It was a lot safer being on her side.

Rebecca nodded solemnly. "Sorry," she whispered. Then she looked down at her glass of Coke as if she were dreadfully ashamed.

Alexa smiled with relief and heaved an exhausted sigh.

Being friends with Rebecca Lake was sure taking a lot of hard work.

7

Priscilla stepped into the River Gallery and looked quickly around. Adam had not yet arrived.

She sighed. Maybe he wouldn't show. He couldn't possibly be all that interested in art. Of course in a very short while he'd probably discover he wasn't too interested in her, either.

Priscilla stopped to idly inspect a pair of ceramic candlesticks. What were she and Adam going to talk about, anyway? She sighed. Everything had been so much easier when she thought she was smart. She could chat about anything. Thoughts just flowed. But, now . . .

Priscilla proceeded around the gallery, gazing absentmindedly at the exhibit. A sunny landscape caught her eye for just a moment. A child and her doll perched in a rocking chair grabbed her attention, but only momentarily. Then, suddenly, she stopped.

The piece was breathtaking.

It was a sort of Caribbean jungle scene done in rich pastels. The greens were so deep and smooth, the flowers so . . .

"Hi . . . " Adam's soft voice came wafting toward her from behind.

Priscilla turned to acknowledge him and then looked back at the painting. So, he was here.

Now what?

"Tell me about this," he said softly, respecting the mood of the gallery as people with hushed voices made their way from piece to piece.

Priscilla bit down on her lower lip. She had things to say. She did. But she was afraid. What if she sounded foolish? What if he asked a question she couldn't answer?

And what if she sounded smart here, but later he found out?

"Ummm . . . " Priscilla hesitated.

"The colors are nice. . . . " Adam began. "Is this an oil painting?"

"No, no," Priscilla shook her head. "This is pastels. The artist used a very hard stroke with special soft pastels. She also did a lot of blending."

Priscilla looked down at her purple sneakers. Had she explained that all right? She probably sounded like a phony. Like a "Ms. Know It All About Art."

"It looks like an oil," Adam replied. "That's interesting. I thought pastels were softer than this."

"You're thinking maybe of Degas," Priscilla answered almost without thinking. "Those ballet dancers he does. Those are soft. Almost like drawings. But, this" — Priscilla nodded toward the painting — "is more like a Rousseau. His paintings of tropical scenes like this are very well known and those are oils. This painting reminds me of those."

"Tell me more," Adam urged her on. "You know so much. . . ."

"Ummm," Priscilla began as she turned to smile into his blue eyes. This was going really well. Maybe he wouldn't care that she wasn't that smart about school stuff. Maybe it would be enough that she knew so much about . . .

"I can tell you," a familiar voice from behind them whispered confidently. "Notice the way the forest kind of recedes while the animals and flowers seem to come out at you?"

Priscilla turned to discover Rebecca Lake stepping up to Adam Miller's other side.

"Yeah?" Adam nodded. "How did she do that?"

"The use of color," Rebecca proceeded knowledgeably. "The vibrant tones of the flowers and even the richly colored details in the animals' faces give this painting its three-dimensional look."

Priscilla glanced at the painting and then back at Adam.

"I see . . . " he nodded, turning to smile at Rebecca with what looked like admiration.

Priscilla stepped slightly away and pretended to study the painting. She couldn't talk like that. She could never sound like such an . . . intellectual.

She didn't have the vocabulary.

She didn't have the smarts.

"Do you agree?" Adam asked her softly, touching her hand slightly with his own.

Priscilla nodded stiffly. "Sure."

Adam pointed to the still life hanging next to the jungle scene. "And this one?"

Priscilla looked at Rebecca expectantly.

"Well," Rebecca began, leaning in toward the work.

Priscilla stood there quietly, somberly, studiously, as Rebecca delivered a speech on the painting before them. Something about the placement. The mood. The shadows.

She'd never hated someone as much in her whole life.

"I see," Adam nodded, flashing Priscilla a pleased and satisfied smile.

Priscilla nodded as if to signal her agreement.

And then she imagined what exactly it would feel like to take that still life and smash it directly over Rebecca's head.

The placement. The mood. The shadows.

It would truly be a work of art.

Saturday evening, Priscilla stared down at her spaghetti and meatballs, filled with rage. This was ridiculous. How much could a person take? First algebra, then Rebecca, and now this?

"Robert, there are a few gifted programs I've found out about. We need to go over them" — Mrs. Levitt paused and smiled broadly — "I'm so proud of you."

"My son," Jon Levitt chimed in, thumping his chest with an open palm.

Priscilla looked across the table at her father blankly.

"Isn't it marvelous?" Mr. Levitt asked her. "One child is wonderfully talented! The other is wonderfully smart! How lucky can we get!"

"Not much luckier," Priscilla muttered. "It's like heaven around here."

"She's just jealous," Robert chuckled. He puffed out his chest. "I'm a genius."

"Oh, please," Priscilla snapped. "You're also a jerk."

"Priscilla! Do not refer to your brother in that way," Mrs. Levitt protested. "I don't know what your problem is, but if you have something to say, try saying it nicely." She turned to her son. "A little humility would do you good, Robert."

Priscilla popped the meatball into her mouth

and stared at her mother challengingly. Ms. Never Understand Anything. She had nothing to say to her. In fact, not to anyone.

She'd hardly been able to say good-bye to Adam after the gallery. What had she mumbled to him dejectedly as they parted? She couldn't even re-member.

"Well, speaking of which," her father broke into the silence, "how are things going for you at school, honey? How did you do on that algebra test?" He smiled at her warmly and then took a sip from his water glass.

Priscilla continued chewing on the meatball. Who did he think he was fooling with that casual act? He was always disappointed when she got bad grades. She could feel it. He was a history professor at Columbia University. How could he not be?

"I did okay," Priscilla lied. They didn't have to know. She could switch classes without letting on. They trusted her.

That came in handy.

"So . . . " Robert piped up with a big grin. "What d'ya get?"

"None of your business," Priscilla snapped. "You are really getting on my nerves. Just keep your mouth shut, okay?"

"Fine, fine," Robert held up both his hands. "That bad, huh?"

Priscilla was about to snap something back when, instead, she covered her face with both her hands. There was a deafening silence in the room.

"Enough, Robert. Are you through?" Mr. Levitt asked pointedly.

"Yes, sir," Robert responded quickly and quietly. He stood up, placing his napkin on the table. "I was just kidding around," he muttered.

"Yes," Mr. Levitt nodded with an insincere smile.

As the dining room door swung closed behind Robert, Priscilla squirmed miserably in her chair.

"What's going on with you at school, dear?" Mrs. Levitt began. "You can tell us."

Priscilla shrugged. She hated this. Really hated this. "Nothing to worry about." She tried to smile. It didn't work.

"I think that's not true," Mr. Levitt continued. "You've always done well in school. . . . "

"Nothing's forever," Priscilla snapped suddenly. She looked from her father to her mother. She was a terrible liar. "You said it yourself, anyway. Robert's the smart one."

"We didn't mean that you weren't smart," Mrs. Levitt insisted. "Only that you each have different gifts."

"Right," Priscilla nodded sarcastically. "Well, I got a D on my algebra test. Some brain. And a

C+ on my last book report." She paused and smiled at her parents. "Now what do you say?"

"I'd say you'd better buckle down, young lady," Mrs. Levitt replied curtly.

"You probably need some help with the way you're studying," Mr. Levitt commented evenly. "Lots of students with straight A's in high school do poorly their freshman year in college because they haven't adjusted to the demands of a new school. It may be the same for you."

"Or it may be that I'm not that . . . that . . . smart," Priscilla whispered. She could feel the tears welling up in her eyes.

"You know, math was never your strong suit," Mrs. Levitt offered matter-of-factly. "You need to give it special time."

"But that's just it!" Priscilla suddenly exploded. "I'm not smart at ANYTHING this year!" The tears were now trickling down her cheeks. "It's so embarrassing! And now I'm supposed to go into the slower algebra class and I feel so humiliated!" She covered her eyes with her hands. "I'm not even the best artist in the school anymore! Someone else is really good!"

"Jealousy is not a pretty sight, Priscilla. Besides, did it ever occur to you that whoever this person is might be jealous of you?" Mrs. Levitt offered evenly.

"Right," Priscilla snapped sarcastically. Fat chance.

"You have too much pride," Mrs. Levitt continued solemnly. "No one is great at everything. The new class will probably be good for you. Besides, where's your faith in yourself?"

"Joan . . . " Mr. Levitt interrupted his wife, "I can understand why Priscilla might . . . "

"Want to disappear?" Priscilla finished his sentence. She pushed back her chair. "Maybe that's because you'd like to also? Pretty embarrassing, isn't it? Having a daughter in the SLOW class." She said the word "slow" very loudly. She dragged out the "O" sound for effect.

"I'm not embarrassed in the least," Mr. Levitt insisted. "Believe me."

"I don't!" Priscilla cried out. "May I be excused, please?" she asked in a shaking voice.

"You may," Mrs. Levitt replied evenly. "But understand your father and I expect to see an improvement."

Priscilla nodded. "I know that." Abruptly, she pushed back her chair and rushed out of the dining room. Racing up the stairs, the tears began to fall in a steady stream down her cheeks.

Sure, her parents expected better. So did she! But what difference did that make!

Reaching her room, Priscilla slammed the door behind her and sank into her desk chair. Placing her head in her hands, she waited for the tears to subside.

She waited to feel like herself again. She waited.

And waited.

But nothing happened. This new, this awful Priscilla, had simply seemed to move in.

Just like Rebecca had. Quickly, quietly, and everywhere.

Her mother was right. Where was her faith in herself? Was it just gone? Forever? It felt like she'd lost her most special, very best friend.

She was so impossibly lonely . . . and embarrassed.

Idly she opened her notebook, only to spot the latest English assignment: "Create a poem that reflects an innermost feeling."

Priscilla sighed unhappily. This used to be her favorite kind of assignment. Words used to just happen.

She reached for a pencil. Then she turned to a blank page, took a deep trembling breath, and sat perfectly still.

Nothing was coming.

Not that she didn't know her innermost feeling. It was simply too horrible to write about. Finally, almost as if it had a life of its own, her pencil began to move across the paper.

There was a time when I could see
All the terrific things in me

But now I think I've lost that sight,
And now I say "Was I ever right?"

She paused. Done.
Not that she'd ever, in a million years, show it
to a soul.

8

Alexa leaned back against Stephanie's basement wall Sunday afternoon and watched as Rebecca, hair bouncing, arms swaying, feet stomping, demonstrated a new dance.

Behind her a line of five excited, laughing, extremely captivated girls followed her every move.

It was a nauseating sight.

And it was not an especially electrifying dance step, either.

Alexa picked up a lock of her thick blonde hair and began looking for split ends. When would it be time to leave? Her father would be driving up any minute.

Alexa glanced up toward the doorway. Didn't parents look at their watches anymore?

"Come on over!" Rebecca called out, waving toward Alexa.

"Oh! No thanks!" Alexa called back with an exceedingly, almost painfully, bright smile. "I know it already!" She paused. "You go on!" She picked up another lock of hair. Right. That was all she needed.

Create a scene in which someone else was showing HER how to do something cool. Alexa the follower?

No way.

"Rebecca, you are so good at this!" Julie cried out.

"The best," Stephanie agreed loudly.

Alexa grimaced. She flung her head back and tried to enjoy the feel of her healthy long hair swaying against her back.

She could dance, too. She stole a glance at Rebecca.

Maybe not quite as well as her, but who cared.

Her eyes traveled up and down the line of smiling, twisting, turning, girls.

Well, actually, maybe they did.

And it just wouldn't do.

A half hour before dinnertime, Alexa lay on her bed, trying to decide. She stared at the lavender-and-green floral wallpaper border that wove its way about the bedroom ceiling.

Rebecca Lake.

Such a beautiful girl. So lively. So exciting.

So awfully, horribly, equal to her own star power.

It just wasn't fun. Not the way she'd thought it would be.

Alexa swung both feet to the floor and reached for her phone.

When was the last time she'd had to do this? Call around. Take a kind of survey. Actually worry about where she stood against some other girl?

Not since the end of seventh grade. When she'd heard that her ex-best friend, Ms. Brains herself, Vivienne Bennis, had been saying perfectly awful things about her. Spreading lies, in fact, about her sincerity, her loyalty, her sense of fair play.

Not that Vivienne had been COMPLETELY wrong.

Just, well, out of line. And looking at things from a very narrow perspective. After all, who was sincere, loyal, and fair ALL the time?

Well, whatever. It was that time again. Who knew? Maybe everyone was just pretending to like Rebecca. If they were, why waste any more time? Rebecca was just too, well, fabulous to take. Alexa grimaced. Of course, on the other hand, if Rebecca was gaining in popularity, she'd just have to keep at it. Be her best friend.

No matter how miserable it felt.

Alexa cleared her throat and dialed Julie's number.

She grabbed a pencil and piece of paper. On the top she scrawled in giant red letters:

Julie answered after the first ring.

"Hi, there!" Alexa began cheerfully. She paused. Small talk would be best, first.

"Did you enjoy today?" She began doodling in a corner of the paper, one heart after another.

Julie hesitated. "Sure. Why? Didn't you?"

Alexa frowned. Small talk was a bore.

"So, tell me, what do you think of this Rebecca Lake?" Alexa asked. She began printing tiny A's and M's inside each heart.

"Huh? Like, what do you mean?" Julie asked lightly.

What was it with Julie today? Everything was a question. Hadn't she heard? A person answered questions with answers.

"Well, what do you think of her? Do you like her? Do you think she's nice. For real?"

"Oh, yes," Julie practically gushed. "In fact, I tried to get her to come over today, but she said she had too much homework. Did you hear she got a 90 on the history quiz? She's been with us a week and she got a 90?" Julie sighed. "Some people just have it all."

Alexa cringed. That's what people were supposed to think about *her*. Alexa Craft. Not Rebecca. Of course how was she supposed to compete with the grades? Not that she was dumb. Not at all. But she did have to work to do well.

And that took time. Too much time.

What about her looks? Her boyfriends? Her friends? Her tennis? Her nails?

Really, the list was endless.

"You don't like her?" Julie asked curiously.

"Oh, NO!" Alexa exclaimed loudly. Defensively. Almost fearfully. "Of course not! Don't say that! I like her a lot." Alexa paused. "We're close. I was just wondering how you felt, because, well, you know, she's new and a little worried about how everyone feels, so I said I'd check it out."

Julie chuckled. "Well, tell her I'm crazy about her. Okay? And so are Pam and Laurie, too. In fact, everyone is!"

Alexa nodded into the phone. "Sure thing. Oh! I just checked my watch. I promised my mother I'd do an errand. See you!" And with that, Alexa Craft practically slammed the receiver down.

A second later, the phone began to ring. Irritably, she grabbed for it. "Yes?" she barked.

"Nice," Mac replied, chuckling softly.

"Oh . . . oh . . . sorry," Alexa quickly softened her voice as she willed herself to calm down. "Hi, Mac!"

"Listen," he said, talking quickly. Almost nervously. "Instead of shopping for that racquet, you know this little carnival or something is going to be in the park Tuesday for some charity. It's just for a few days. And I thought you might like to come with me. It has a small Ferris wheel, and a merry-go-round, and bumper cars. That kind of thing . . . "

"Oh, I'd love to . . . " Alexa breathed softly in her best low, sexy voice. Okay. This was a real improvement. Mac was calling for a date only days since he'd last seen her. It was romantic, too. Much better than tennis shopping. They'd be sitting very close on the Ferris wheel. It would be so . . .

"And I was thinking," Mac continued, "that I'd bring my friend Randy Stern, and you could bring Rebecca."

Alexa paused. How come this had to involve Rebecca? And since when was Mac so interested in matchmaking? She could feel her excitement melting away. Actually, shopping for a tennis racquet felt like an invitation to go steady next to this.

"Hello?" Mac said in confusion. "Are you there?"

"Yes . . . I am," Alexa began haltingly. "I'm not sure if Rebecca is busy or not."

"Oh, well Randy would like to meet her, and I thought that since you two were such good friends, it would be cool. You know. All of us, together."

Alexa nodded. Yes, she did know. She just wasn't quite sure what she knew. Or if she wanted to know it.

"Okay . . . " she replied slowly. "I'll give her a call. . . . "

"Great!" Mac exclaimed.

"Yeah," Alexa replied dryly.

"I'm looking forward to doing this with you," Mac added a little awkwardly. Or insincerely.

Alexa couldn't tell.

"Me, too," Alexa said unhappily. "Bye-bye."

She placed the receiver down and stared at the wall for a long while.

What was Rebecca's phone number? She didn't remember.

She looked around the room. Where was her phone book?

She just didn't know.

Of course there was always the operator. But that cost fifty cents. Her parents hated that.

Oh, well.

Then, again, if she didn't call, maybe Mac would cancel.

Alexa glanced down at the top of her history notebook where she had first penned Rebecca's phone number.

Ah, yes. How fortunate.

And to think she'd almost forgotten . . .

Her eyes moved to the piece of paper upon

which she'd written the words THE REBECCA
TEMPERATURE.

Picking up her pencil, she slowly and resignedly
scrawled two words across the page:

TOO HOT

9

"Aren't you a little nervous for Michelle?" Gina whispered Monday afternoon to Priscilla as they took their seats in the auditorium. She wiggled her shoulders. "I'm sure she'll do great."

Priscilla nodded absentmindedly and glanced with discomfort at Vivienne, who was seated to her right. Tomorrow was Tuesday. Why hadn't she told them yet about her new class? What did she think?

They wouldn't notice? Wouldn't care?

Wouldn't secretly think terrible things . . .

She ran a finger along the delicate lines of her drawing, which graced the cover of the recital program. A keyboard design seemed to wrap like a ribbon around the flute's long narrow casing.

"Nice art," Gina whispered in Priscilla's ear.

Priscilla smiled. She looked up at Gina tentatively. "Thanks," she said softly.

They were still close. She could sense it. If only she could have told her this weekend about the algebra class. Just called her and blurted it out.

But she couldn't. Not with Rebecca in the picture.

Her position was too unclear. Too fragile.

"A lot of people came," Margo commented, turning around from the seat directly in front of Priscilla's.

"Well, what do you expect?" Vivienne chimed in softly. "We're practically popular. Remember? Michelle has a lot of friends." She smiled. "Besides. Robin is playing the piano, you know. Alexa probably paid people to come. . . . "

"Oh, wow! Look who just walked in!" Margo cried out. "Rebecca Lake!"

"Oh, great! Over here!" Vivienne whirled around and immediately started waving her hands in the air. She pointed to the empty seat on her other side.

Priscilla buried her face in the program. She studied the names of the performers. She recited over and over the pieces they would play. She tried desperately to shut out the conversation that was spinning around her. . . .

"I can't believe you came!" Vivienne exclaimed.

"I wouldn't have missed it," Rebecca insisted.

"Lots of people don't like these events," Margo declared. "We came for Michelle."

"That's why I came," Rebecca replied, as if it were a given.

As if she belonged. As if she, too, had a responsibility to their good friend.

Priscilla cringed. She felt a tap on her shoulder.

"Mind moving over one?" Rebecca asked softly. She pointed to the seat next to Vivienne. "It's kind of broken."

Filled with resentment, Priscilla turned to look at Gina.

"Sure," Gina responded sweetly. With no apparent resentment. Priscilla stood up silently and followed Gina, like a puppy dog, as they slid down the aisle one place. She watched jealously as Rebecca settled into the seat between herself and Vivienne. Smugly. Contentedly.

It felt disgusting.

She glanced at the empty seat next to Margo's. Why couldn't Rebecca have sat there? Why did Priscilla have to move?

In fact, why had she moved? What was the matter with her!?

Miserably, she watched as Pamela Brady slid through the aisle and planted herself in the seat Rebecca had just vacated. She watched as Pamela put down her books, settled back, and began chatting with Margo.

She watched as Pamela wiggled in the seat, turned in the seat, and almost bounced in the seat, which didn't shake, or tremble, or creak, or look broken in any way at all.

"Rebecca!" a strong, insistent voice broke through the din of the crowd's chatter. Priscilla looked up to find Alexa motioning eagerly at the end of the row. "Come join us!" She pointed to Mona and Julie, who were sitting across the aisle with two empty seats between them. "We saved you a seat!"

For a long moment, everyone was silent.

Rebecca cleared her throat, her eyes darting back and forth between Alexa and Vivienne.

Priscilla looked down at her lap and held her breath. This was too good to be true. Was it possible? Was Rebecca going to choose Alexa? In another moment, could this part of the nightmare be over? If she chose Alexa, the crowd would never vote her in. Never.

She waited, filled with hope.

With Rebecca gone, she could get through tomorrow.

Sure, it would be a little tricky, but . . .

Suddenly the auditorium began to darken.

Priscilla turned back toward Rebecca, who was now smiling brightly. At everyone.

"How can I?" she whispered in Alexa's direction. She pointed to the stage, upon which Michelle was now walking. Then Rebecca flashed a warm, happy smile at Vivienne, and settled back in her seat.

"Boy, that was close. . . . " Gina whispered in

Priscilla's ear. "For a second there, I thought she'd chose Alexa and not us. . . . "

Priscilla hesitated.

Was Gina kidding? She called that a decision? Had she been asleep or something?

Rebecca hadn't chosen anyone.

The lights had dimmed. There was no time to move.

She hadn't taken a stand at all.

But, then, Priscilla realized with a dull ache, really, neither had she. She was just too afraid of their disapproval. Their suspicions. Their rejection.

"Ms. Michelle Greene and Ms. Robin Montgomery will now play a jazz duet by . . . "

Priscilla sighed deeply as the voice droned on. She sank into her chair as the rhythmic, spirited tones began to float toward her. She listened as Michelle and Robin, both with feeling and skill, spun their melodies, each weaving through the other. She closed her eyes. The music was so alive. It was as if two little children were dancing, laughing, skipping about each other in a sparkling field, never quite touching, but reaching toward one another and then gently pulling away.

She could feel her sullen mood lifting ever so slightly.

A moment later, Margo turned around and quickly pressed a folded piece of paper into her hand. Priscilla's name was scrawled across the front in Vivienne's unmistakable handwriting.

Opening it, she read the message with a sinking heart:

Time is running out. Alexa is pushing. Rebecca is ours. Let's vote tomorrow.

Priscilla refolded the sheet and placed it in her pocket.

So that was that.

Starting tomorrow, nothing would ever be the same.

Monday evening Alexa pulled out the bottom drawer of her bureau. It had to be here somewhere. That black cotton turtleneck.

That Rebecca kind of thing.

Her hand found the tip of its sleeve and angrily she pulled it out. Black was definitely not her best color. Not this close to her face, anyway. Holding the shirt up by its shoulders, Alexa tried to imagine how she would look tomorrow.

Besides dead.

Quickly she pulled it on, grabbed a pair of faded blue jeans and, holding her breath, threw open the closet door to study herself in the mirror.

Alexa gazed at her reflection with a critical eye. Definitely not half-bad. Something was missing, though. Something else Rebecca-ish, but she couldn't figure out what it was.

She tilted her head to one side. Then the other. Then she thought of it.

Reaching for her jewelry box, she started scrounging around madly for a pair of earrings that would flicker, dance, make a statement, just as Rebecca's always did.

She couldn't find them. Hers were more delicate. Refined.

Boring.

Mac would yawn his way to Rebecca's door.

Alexa grabbed the phone and started dialing.

"Robin," she began, urgently, almost feverishly, when she heard her friend's voice. "Don't you have a pair of really wild earrings? You know that pair your parents brought back from Mexico?"

"Sure," Robin hesitated. "Ummm. I'm not really supposed to lend those out."

"But you have to!" Alexa cried out. "I'm seeing Mac tomorrow, and we're going with Rebecca and Randy Stern and I have to look really fabulous. I have to look just like . . . "

Alexa caught herself just in time.

What a thing to say. To think. How could she?

Her own good looks weren't good enough? She had to imitate the style of someone else just to keep a guy interested?

Forget it. No way. That wasn't it at all.

"I have to look just like, great," Alexa corrected

herself. Which was really what she meant, she was quite sure.

"Well . . . okay," Robin caved in. "But be careful with them."

"I will . . . " Alexa responded absentmindedly, clearly never doubting for a moment that Robin would cave in. She walked with the phone back to the mirror and flicked her hair from side to side thoughtfully.

She certainly wouldn't do it. Buy the dye or anything.

But, still, it was fun to imagine.

She'd have looked great as a brunette, too.

Having nothing to do with Rebecca, of course.

10

"**O**kay, are we all ready for the meeting?" Vivienne asked excitedly Tuesday morning. She clasped both her hands together. "It's a big, big day."

Priscilla looked down at her fuchsia glitter sneakers. It sure was. In another few minutes, the bell would ring, math period would begin, and everyone would know.

She just couldn't cut it.

"I'm ready!" Gina sighed happily.

"Me, too," Michelle said softly. Thoughtfully. "It feels strange, though. We've been five for a long time."

"And you, Pris?" Vivienne suddenly asked, with a smile on her face and tension in her voice.

Priscilla closed her eyes for a brief moment. Why did she feel like hitting someone? What did Vivienne think? That Rebecca was going to somehow change her life? Make her beautiful? Exciting? Unbeatable? Just turn every last thing into magic?

She looked around at the other Crowd members. Did they honestly think that, too? And if they did, why didn't she?

Was she really that impossibly jealous?

That insanely insecure?

She sighed heavily. The old Priscilla might have known. But this one . . . this one was too afraid to stand up for herself. Too scared to insist they slow down. Too confused to believe in herself.

"Ready," Priscilla finally replied.

This Priscilla felt as if she were hanging on to the Crowd by the slimmest, most delicate thread in the world.

She checked her watch again. The bell would ring any second.

There had to be a way to just sneak into Ms. Williams' class and avoid the explanations. She'd get to them later. At the meeting or something.

Suddenly the class bell ripped through the air.

"Let's go!" Margo waved her arm through the air. "Tally-ho!"

Gina, Vivienne, Michelle, and Margo began walking toward Mrs. Simon's door.

Priscilla stood perfectly still in the center of the hallway. Ms. Williams' class was in the opposite direction. She'd wait. She'd wait until they'd all entered Mrs. Simon's class and the door closed behind them. Then, quickly, she'd scoot into Ms. Williams' class. And that would be that.

In an incomplete, abrupt, cowardly kind of way.

"Priscilla! Are you coming?" Gina called out softly, her head peeking around from Mrs. Simon's door.

"Yeah," Viv appeared in the doorway. "You're not angry about anything, are you?"

"Trouble between such good friends?" Alexa called out from a few feet behind Priscilla. "Hard to believe!" She turned to Rebecca, who was walking beside her. "Those Practically Terrific People. What would we do without them?"

Priscilla noticed Rebecca try unsuccessfully to stifle a giggle. It made her sick.

Quickly she turned to see if Vivienne had noticed.

She frowned. Vivienne was grinning from ear to ear.

Apparently not. But, then, what else was new?

She waited. Any second Viv and Gina would go back in their math room, and Alexa would be close behind. Why couldn't everyone be in separate classrooms? Like before? When Ms. Korf was still there? Priscilla bent down to retie her purple velvet sneaker lace, which was already tied.

But nobody moved.

Priscilla straightened up. It was the ultimate nightmare. The Practically Popular Crowd at one end of the hallway. Alexa and Rebecca at another. All looking at her.

There was no avoiding it. The curtain had to go up.

Taking a deep and shaky breath, Priscilla turned away from her crowd and started heading toward Ms. Williams' door.

"Priscilla! What are you doing?" Gina called out. "Algebra's in here!"

Priscilla didn't answer. She opened the door to Ms. Williams' class just in time for two other students to rush inside.

"I think she knows that," Alexa called out, loudly. In a singsong voice. "Am I right, Priscilla?"

Priscilla hesitated. She turned and looked down the hall at her friends. Her crowd. One by one they'd each walked out of the classroom and were now standing in the hallway.

"Having a little trouble with school?" Alexa continued mockingly.

"Oh, shush up," Vivienne called out angrily. "Listen, Alexa, the only reason you haven't flunked out yet is because Robin and Mona let you copy off their papers. Who do you think you're kidding?" Vivienne smiled sweetly at Rebecca. "Certainly not our new classmate!"

Priscilla smiled meekly in Vivienne's direction. Good ole Viv. In a pinch, Vivienne would fight any battle on behalf of a friend.

"I . . . I . . . can't believe you said that," Alexa cried out, moving quickly toward Mrs. Simon's class. She shot Rebecca a nervous glance. "VIVIENNE BENNIS, YOU HAVE GONE TOO FAR!"

Vivienne shrugged. "So sue me." She looked down the hall at Priscilla. "We'll see you later, okay?" She smiled sympathetically. "It's okay, Priscilla," she added. And then she and the rest of The Practically Popular Crowd disappeared into the classroom.

Priscilla stepped into Ms. Williams' classroom and shut the door behind her. An unbearable rush of loneliness suddenly enveloped her.

She looked around the room. About twenty students were looking at her with surprise.

She stared back.

So this was what the dumb group looked like. Funny. They looked normal.

"It's okay, Priscilla." Vivienne's words echoed in her mind.

But it wasn't okay. This would never be okay.

Priscilla slipped into an empty chair and looked around once more. It was the oddest feeling. The Practically Popular Crowd in one place, her in another. Certainly they didn't do everything together. But they'd never been forced apart. Placed on two levels. They'd always felt equal . . . in different ways.

This had never happened before.

The Crowd traveled together. A member didn't get left behind.

And if she did . . .

"Hi," a soft voice whispered.

Priscilla looked up to find Carol Stedman sitting in the next chair. She nodded swiftly and then turned away.

She didn't want to get friendly with people here. She wasn't staying. She wasn't like them. Or was she?

Priscilla could feel the tears once again welling up.

She covered her face with both hands for the briefest moment.

How was she going to face the Crowd this afternoon? How?

She looked up at the blackboard. A single simple equation rested upon it. Priscilla tried to concentrate. Tried to get it.

Suddenly she did. $x = 4$.

A tear began to make its way down her cheek.

Four. The new number of REAL Practically Popular Crowd members.

Of course not for long. Once again she picked up her pencil.

$4 + x = 5$

Priscilla grimaced.

"x = Rebecca" she scrawled with such intense resentment that the pencil point broke and skittered noiselessly to the floor.

11

"Isn't this great!" Rebecca whispered in Alexa's ear as they stood in line at the bumper cars. "It's really romantic, don't you think?" She motioned towards Randy, who was now standing off to the side chatting amiably with Mac. "He's just what I had in mind."

Alexa nodded gloomily. Why had she worn this black shirt? She studied Rebecca's bright purple pullover.

Suddenly Rebecca was into color?

When had that happened?

"You're so quiet. What's up?" Rebecca asked curiously. "You and Mac look cool together. He's crazy about you!"

"Yeah?" Alexa replied, perking up considerably. She squared her shoulders and turned to flash Rebecca a big smile. Time to shape up. Look how great Rebecca was being! It wasn't Rebecca's fault she was feeling so competitive.

Friends were supposed to keep that under control.

Of course it didn't help that Rebecca was being so charming with Randy *and* Mac. So witty. So much, well, FUN.

Sure, she'd cut Alexa off a few times, which was naturally annoying. But that had probably just been because of her nerves. She was new to the group. People talked too much when they got nervous. . . .

"Hey, guys!" Alexa called out, impulsively leaning over to pull Mac's sleeve. After all, she could turn on the charm, too. "We're lonely over here!"

"Right," Mac chuckled. "Give us a second, though, okay? Randy's got some problem with his basketball game I'm talking to him about. . . . "

"Oh, sure," Rebecca leapt in loudly. She grabbed Alexa's hand. "Come on. Let's give them a chance to talk. It looks important." She nodded at the two boys. "Alexa didn't mean to be pushy."

Alexa stared at Rebecca openmouthed as she allowed herself to be pulled back into line.

"I . . . I . . . wasn't being pushy," Alexa stammered with disbelief. "How could you have said that?"

"Don't be silly," Rebecca whispered earnestly. "I was helping. Guys like girls who appreciate they need special time alone. Trust me. . . . "

"But I wasn't being pushy," Alexa protested. "You shouldn't have . . ."

"I had to," Rebecca replied warmly. Supportively. "You didn't see the look Mac gave you. What I said was important. I saved you. He'll forgive you."

Alexa stared at Rebecca numbly. With deep confusion.

And just a touch of uncertain gratitude.

How nice. She'd saved her. He'd forgive her.

But as hard as Alexa tried, she just couldn't figure out what it was she'd done.

Priscilla stood off to the side, watching the gay and colorful carnival. She checked her watch. It was almost time for the meeting at Vivienne's.

She grimaced at the thought of walking into Vivienne's room with all those eyes upon her.

Waiting. Questioning. Accusing.

How come you're in Ms. Williams' class?

Where were you all afternoon?

You don't want to vote Rebecca in, do you? She's just too talented for you, isn't she?

Priscilla could hear the carousel music pumping out its cheerful waltz. UM PAH PAH, UM PAH PAH, UM PAH PAH.

Over and over it played, while the children below laughed and the parents chased after them, and . . .

Priscilla stepped away from the tree she'd been leaning against to take a better look.

And Rebecca and Alexa stood side by side like the closest friends in the world.

"This is pretty nice," Mac said, slipping his arm briefly around Alexa's shoulder as they slid into the bumper car.

Alexa snuggled up against him, enjoying the feel of his soft green-and-blue flannel shirt. "It is . . . " she whispered. "I could sit here forever." Then she hesitated.

Was that too pushy? She couldn't tell.

Mac grinned.

Alexa heaved a sigh of relief.

"Ready?" Randy called out from a bumper car a few yards away.

"You bet!" Mac cried out. "Rebecca, you'd better hang on! I'm a wild man!"

"Well, I'm a wild girl!" Rebecca shouted back gleefully.

Alexa smiled as Mac threw back his head and burst out laughing.

It was so nice seeing Mac having so much fun. Being so spirited. Feeling so good.

Too bad it had nothing to do with her.

How come he hadn't told her to watch out? Told her he was a wild man? Given her a chance to be witty and fabulously terrific?

"Alexa, are you scared?" Rebecca called out joyfully.

"Of course not," Alexa shot back. Her chance had come.

"Not with Mac here!" she continued. "I predict he'll lead us to victory," she said, raising both her hands in the air.

Yes. Good work. A very funny comeback.

"You're probably right!" Rebecca suddenly called back as she playfully covered Randy's mouth with her hand.

"What a kick she is," Mac chuckled, grabbing hold of the wheel with a wild gleam in his eye.

Alexa shrugged. "That's why we're friends," she said feebly, only dimly aware that that had nothing to do with it at all.

Priscilla walked over to a vendor, purchased a can of soda, and sat down on a bench. She closed her eyes.

It would be a disaster. The Practically Popular Crowd could not afford to have a member who was that close to Alexa. It would compromise their privacy. Their trust.

Their everything.

If only Rebecca hadn't come along now. Just when Priscilla was at her weakest. She could have slowed things down. Convinced the Crowd they were moving too fast. Stood her ground.

Rebecca wasn't right for them. She was sure of it.

Even if she was horribly jealous.

Priscilla, almost completely hidden by the passersby, watched while Alexa, Mac, Rebecca, and Randy banged away at each other in their bumper cars. Laughing. Calling each other names. Behaving as if they owned the place.

She sighed. They had it all.

She used to feel like that, too.

A long, long time ago.

"So should we sit down and have something to eat?" Randy asked, taking Rebecca's hand in the process.

"Good idea," Mac replied, slipping his arm through Alexa's. "Let's see . . . " His eyes circled the nearby area. "We can get hot dogs over here, and fruit juice over there." He pointed to a stand on the other side of the carousel.

"Actually, I'd just like a frozen yogurt," Rebecca said softly, as if she were embarrassed. "I have to watch what I eat."

Alexa looked up at the sky.

Being with someone who played the same sort of games she did was certainly sickening.

"Why?" both Mac and Randy asked at the same time.

"Oh, you know . . . " Rebecca giggled coyly.

"I'm sure they do," Alexa volunteered sarcastically. She wrapped her arms around Mac's neck. "How about you and I go get the drinks and they can get the food and we'll meet back here?"

"Good idea," Mac answered softly. He cupped Alexa's chin in his hand and lightly kissed her on the lips. "Let's go," he said invitingly.

Alexa smiled up at him alluringly, meaningfully, she hoped, and then unwrapped herself from around his neck. Slipping her hand through Mac's, she began to gently pull him toward the fruit stand.

"Long line," Mac grumbled as they arrived.

Alexa slipped her arm through his and moved close. "It's okay," she said.

"Oh, look!" Mac suddenly cried out. "Over there! Someone just pushed into Rebecca and she dropped her yogurt. I wonder if she has enough money for another? She's waving at us. I'll be right back."

And a second later, Mac disappeared into the crowd that had formed around the carousel.

Alexa turned back to face the fruit stand.

How nice of Mac. A damsel in distress, and there he was.

Poor Rebecca, losing her yogurt and all.

Alexa bit down on her lower lip very hard.

Okay. So what if Mac had a little crush on Rebecca? It was natural. She was new. It would pass. Rebecca would set him straight.

That's what best friends did for each other.

Even Alexa wouldn't double-cross a really good friend.

Which said a lot, since she and Rebecca were so much alike.

Weren't they?

Priscilla stood up and began circling the little carnival.

It was definitely time to go.

She smiled as a little child rushed past her, a cloud of pink and blue balloons clutched in one hand.

"Excuse me," Priscilla said softly as she brushed past a couple who were standing perfectly still beside a concession stand, lost in a serious and long kiss.

Sadly, filled with bittersweet feelings of longing, Priscilla turned to glance at them. To admire their love. Their tenderness. Their closeness.

Her thoughts turned to Adam.

Her eyes widened.

Boy, things changed quickly in Port Andrews.

Alexa and Mac were supposed to be an item.

So why were Rebecca's lips planted so firmly where Alexa's should have been?

"Thanks for getting me a new yogurt," Rebecca said, smiling sweetly at Mac as she took another lick from her cone.

"No problem," Mac informed her matter-of-factly.

Alexa took another sip of her orange juice and then placed her hand over Mac's, which was now resting lightly on her knee. Rebecca was right. It was nice of Mac.

And Mona was wrong. She did like Mac. A lot, in fact.

"So what do we do now?" Alexa asked, smiling around at everyone.

"Well, I've got some homework I've got to do," Randy replied. He checked his watch. "I'm going to have to get going."

"That reminds me," Rebecca said, shaking her head with disgust. "That was really lousy what Vivienne said about you in the hallway, Alexa."

Alexa froze. Why did Rebecca keep doing this? Embarrassing her? In such supportive ways?

"What did she do?" Mac asked curiously.

"Oh, nothing," Alexa said quickly. She shook her head in Rebecca's direction.

"Nothing! Why, she accused Alexa of copying homework from everyone. That's not nothing!" Rebecca cried out with indignation.

Alexa cringed. Rebecca had to be out of her mind.

That was it. She wasn't mean. Or nasty. No. Just crazy.

"Enough, Rebecca," Alexa snapped. "Thanks,

but I can handle it." Then she looked down into her orange juice.

And she would, too.

Vivienne would pay.

Someone had to.

Rebecca, her very dearest friend, was making her mad enough to spit.

12

Priscilla stood quietly outside of Vivienne's bedroom door. Anxiously she scrunched the rim of her floppy purple felt hat.

She was late.

She could hear the voices inside now. She tried to listen in for her name. But all she heard was something about Rebecca. Rebecca's dress. Rebecca's hair. She closed her eyes for a moment. Rebecca this. Rebecca that. She was SO sick of Rebecca.

And so tired of feeling left out.

How could she hope to compete? What did she have now that made her stand out? It certainly wasn't her art. Not anymore. Rebecca had that. She touched her hat once more.

Of course Rebecca didn't exactly have Priscilla's quirky sense of style. . . .

Priscilla impulsively squared her shoulders. The old Priscilla. She had to be there somewhere.

She was colorful. Creative. Unique. How could those things have just disappeared?

Priscilla reached for the doorknob.

She looked down at her baggy light-blue jeans and silky patchwork blouse with the mismatched gold coin buttons.

She wasn't all THAT replaceable.

Taking a deep breath, she opened the door. "Hi," Priscilla said evenly.

"Look!" Gina, Michelle, Vivienne, and Margo all called out in unison.

Priscilla stood, paralyzed, in the doorway.

Around the neck of each member of the crowd hung a quirky, brightly colored man's tie. Upon each was handpainted an elaborately styled rosebud with a long looping graceful stem, quite unlike the one she'd found in the artroom.

"Aren't they great!" Vivienne cried out. Quickly she picked up a lime-green tie that was resting on the floor. "Here, this is for you! Rebecca said she simply SLAVED over them."

Priscilla nodded and, like a robot, stepped forward to accept it. "Nice," she said. She ran her finger lightly over the rose. Funny. It didn't look or feel handpainted at all.

"Yes," Margo gushed. "I think she might have done it to influence us a little, which really shouldn't happen . . . but, well . . . " She looked around the room at all the smiling faces. "I guess it's working."

"I'm telling you, she's a great addition," Vivienne declared. "She's got pizzazz, she's got talent, she's got originality, she's got brains . . . and she thinks we're great!" She shook her head. "Alexa and her cronies are nothing compared to her."

Priscilla quietly put her books down on Vivienne's blue-and-white-striped comforter and sank to the floor. Hugging her knees to her chest, she looked around the room.

So much for her unique sense of style.

She waited.

Someone was bound to bring up what had happened today. Any second. She looked down at the tie in her hand.

She hated it.

Vivienne suddenly stood up and twirled around. "Does anyone notice anything different about me?"

Priscilla looked her up and down from head to toe.

Nothing.

"My skirt," Vivienne frowned slightly, looking down. "It's shorter than usual. I rolled it up. Rebecca thinks I have nice legs."

Priscilla looked at Vivienne's legs. They were okay. A little bony, though.

She cleared her throat. Okay, a pause was coming. She could feel it. They were going to ask her about Ms. Williams now. Get all sympathetic. Just as long as they kept a lid on it. Didn't go too far . . .

"Anyway," Gina began.

Here it comes, Priscilla thought. She looked at Gina, who smiled at her warmly. Priscilla could feel her stomach tighten. In a second she'd be on. Nervously, she wrapped the tie around her wrist.

"Anyway, can anyone tell me what the answer is to number four in the math homework today because I really tried to figure . . . " Margo's voice suddenly trailed off. Anxiously, she looked around the room and then whispered, "Never mind . . . "

"I guess it's time to call this meeting to order, Viv," Michelle instructed crisply. Too quickly.

Priscilla looked down at the floor.

No one could face her.

It was happening already. Suddenly, there were things they couldn't talk about. Sure, now it was just homework. But they talked about all kinds of things when they studied together. She was going to lose all that. The gap between them would grow. Pretty soon . . .

"Right," Vivienne nodded, picking up her notebook. "I declare this meeting of The Practically Popular Crowd now open. We have important business today," she added, looking around the room. Her eyes settled on Priscilla.

"Let's start with you. Do we vote Rebecca in or out? Give us your opinion. And your reason," Vivienne requested formally.

"I . . . I . . . " Priscilla stammered. "I haven't really given it that much thought. . . . " she began. This was hard to believe. Voting Rebecca in was more important than what had happened to her today? What was going on here?

"Okay, then. Michelle. We'll come back to Priscilla after she's had a chance to think."

"I vote yes," Michelle volunteered. "Because she's got so much going for her and she's a good fit for us. She's special."

Vivienne nodded toward Gina.

"I vote yes," Gina nodded enthusiastically. "I like her. She makes me feel good."

"Me, too," Margo grinned.

Vivienne smiled broadly. "Well, you all know what I think. . . . I think she's great. Smart. Talented. Interesting. Exciting. And cool. I say yes!"

All eyes turned toward Priscilla now.

"We can't vote her in unless everyone agrees," Vivienne reminded her stiffly. "If you check our minutes from last year, that was one of the things we decided . . . in case this day ever came. Maybe you'd like to ask a question or two to help you make up your mind?" She gave Priscilla a challenging look.

Priscilla hesitated. You bet she did. Like, "What's the rush?!" or "What makes you think she isn't the biggest phony you guys ever met?" She bit down on her lower lip thoughtfully.

"Ummmm, well . . . " Priscilla mumbled softly. She looked around the room at all the eager faces. At all the quirky little ties. The ties with all those irritating tiny little R.L.'s painted on them. How could she stop them? She was on shaky enough ground as it was. They hadn't even gotten to ask-. ing her about Ms. Williams' class.

"Okay," she practically whispered. "I say okay."

And maybe it was. Maybe this was all in her head. Her jealous, competitive, prideful head. Yes, accepting Rebecca felt a little like rolling around in poison ivy. But that didn't make it so. Not necessarily.

"YES!" Vivienne called out, raising both fists in the air. "Terrific! Let's call this meeting to a close, and I'll call Rebecca!" Vivienne exclaimed. "She told me she'd be waiting by the phone. Poor thing. She's probably frantic! Oh, and by the way, did I mention? She told me if we voted her in, we could all go with her to look at her father's new offices in that great new building with all the shops in it! Great, huh?!"

"Unbelievable! Let me get on the extension!" Margo laughed. "I'd love to hear her voice!"

"Fine," Vivienne pointed to her door. "There's a phone downstairs in the hallway."

Instantly everyone was on their feet.

Everyone but Priscilla.

Were they kidding? The meeting was over?

But no one had said a word about her. About her humiliation. About not being in their class.

About anything . . .

She watched as Vivienne dialed Rebecca's number.

Was she losing her mind? They all knew how she'd been feeling. Sure, she hadn't told them. But they'd seen the way she'd looked this morning. Sick. Teary. Miserable. Didn't they care?

She watched as Vivienne listened to the phone ring on the other end.

She watched as Vivienne put her finger on the button and dialed again. "Must have been a wrong number," Vivienne murmured. "I just know Rebecca is beside herself, waiting."

Priscilla could feel her eyes brimming over with tears. Her crowd. Her confidantes. Where were they?!

She watched as Vivienne's brow began to wrinkle ever so slightly. "Funny," Vivienne muttered. "She told me she'd be waiting by the phone. . . . "

"Something must have come up," Gina waved it away. "You can't predict what's going to happen."

"She'll be thrilled when she finds out," Margo nodded.

"Absolutely," Michelle agreed.

Priscilla looked around the room with confusion.

Why couldn't they consider the possibility that Rebecca wasn't there, because Rebecca didn't care?

Couldn't they sense Rebecca was trying to steal Priscilla's spot? Didn't that matter?

Priscilla looked around at her Crowd.

They were buzzing about the room, laughing, talking, swinging their ties.

They looked so happy. She had to do something.

"I saw Rebecca with Alexa at that carnival in the park this afternoon," Priscilla blurted out.

"Are you sure?" Gina asked with surprise.

"Of course I am," Priscilla answered stonily.

There was a heavy silence in the room. All eyes turned toward Vivienne.

"Wow . . . " Michelle breathed.

"Boy . . . " Margo added, shaking her head.

"Wow is right," Vivienne suddenly declared, folding her arms across her chest. "If you ask me, we're just in time."

Priscilla could feel her entire body relaxing. A big smile burst forth upon her face. "Yes . . ." She nodded in agreement. Finally her friends understood . . . finally. . . .

"Rebecca needs our protection. She doesn't know what she's doing," Vivienne continued. "You know how we all fell under Alexa's spell at first? Well, what makes Rebecca any different? If you ask me, we're just in time to save her!"

"Right!" Margo, Michelle, and Gina agreed,

bobbing their heads up and down with obvious relief.

"We must be understanding," Gina affirmed.

"Compassionate," Michelle added.

Priscilla picked up her algebra text.

Nothing made sense.

Not algebra. Not this.

But, still, she was sure of two things.

Rebecca had not handpainted one of their ties.

And for reasons she could not quite put her finger on, Priscilla was absolutely positive that The Practically Popular Crowd would live to regret this day.

With or without her.

13

Thursday afternoon, Alexa pulled out her desk chair and sat down. She opened her lavender-colored notebook and picked up a blue felt-tip pen.

Poetry time. She sighed. Such a lot of effort to keep up with Rebecca.

She leaned back in the chair, dropped her head back, and closed her eyes. She could feel her long blonde hair dangling in the air. She shook it and began to speak:

> *"Roses are red*
> *Blonde hair is gold*
> *I know that I look good*
> *'bout sixteen years old."*

Alexa giggled. Then she sat up straight and looked down at the blank page before her. A frown settled on her face.

An inner feeling. Let's see.

Actually, she had loads of them.

She just didn't like sharing them. She hardly liked admitting them to herself.

Alexa began tapping her pencil on the desktop. Hmmm. What was her biggest inner feeling right now?

She closed her eyes.

Anxiety. Rebecca anxiety.

Here she was, knocking herself out for a perfect stranger. It was like she'd gotten caught up in a wild dance and simply couldn't stop. She was just whirling around, getting dizzier and dizzier.

Alexa looked down at the page and impulsively began to write.

Whirling. Whirling ever faster.
That is what I do for show.
Whirling, whirling someplace special
That is where I hope to go.
Whirling, whirling, tell me who I am
That is what I hardly know.

Alexa hesitated, and then wrote the last line:

Except for the very few seconds when I am still.

Letting out a soft sigh, Alexa put her pen down and glanced out the window.

When was she ever still? Hardly ever.

She was just too busy spinning. Whirling. Fearing that she would cease to glitter. That she would lose her charm.

Alexa looked down at her poem and gently, thoughtfully, ran a fingertip under the lines as she recited the words silently. Then she folded the paper in half and placed it in the top drawer of her desk. There was no way she could hand it in. Have it read out loud.

Reveal her inner self so boldly.

That would surely give Rebecca an edge.

With Vivienne Bennis' big-mouth help, of course.

Suddenly Alexa sat up straight, chin high in the air. She scowled. Well, not if she had anything to say about it.

Alexa picked up the phone and began punching numbers.

Payback time.

Rebecca answered on the first ring. "Alexa, hi!" she cried out enthusiastically. "I'm really getting to know your voice. I guess that makes us good friends!" she added.

"Guess so," Alexa sang back, willing herself to mean it. Desperately. "Listen, I was wondering what you're doing Saturday. I thought you might like to go shopping with me." I need to get you alone, she intoned silently. To tell you things. Things that are going to get you awfully mad. At Vivienne. At that stupid crowd.

And more devoted to me.

"Well . . . " Rebecca hesitated. "I'm sort of booked."

"Oh," Alexa frowned. What was she? A concert act? "What are you doing?"

Rebecca giggled almost nervously. Alexa didn't like the way it sounded. False. Uncomfortable. As if she were trying to make something that was most unfunny sound funny. Alexa giggled like that a lot herself. "Actually Vivienne and those girls asked me to go shopping with them, and I just couldn't think of a way to say no, but maybe later we could . . . "

"I suppose," Alexa replied slowly.

Something wasn't right here. Hadn't she said the Crowd got on her nerves? What was she doing shopping with them? Alexa frowned. Then, again, as usual, there was always the more innocent possibility. Maybe she was torn. Maybe she was new and just didn't know who was really "in" and who wasn't.

Well, Alexa would straighten her out. Now.

"Look, Rebecca, you can hang out with whomever you want," she dove in headfirst. There wasn't any point in being subtle. "But I think you should know a few things."

"Oh. Okay," Rebecca said curiously. "What things?"

"Vivienne and her friends are not what they appear to be," Alexa began. She'd start slow.

Something close to the truth. See how it went.

"Like they think they are the only people in the school who are 'together,' if you know what I mean. Which of course couldn't be farther from the truth."

"Well, I know that," Rebecca replied. "You're obviously much more so than they are."

Alexa hesitated. Ordinarily she'd have enjoyed the compliment. But, somehow, from Rebecca, the words felt hollow.

"They are very full of themselves," Alexa continued. Rebecca wasn't annoyed yet. But she'd get her there. "And they are not all that good at getting guys, though they do try to steal a few here and there."

"Fat chance," Rebecca giggled. "Doesn't bother me."

Alexa grimaced. Rebecca wasn't really biting. Something close to honesty wasn't working. Ah, well. This wouldn't be the first time she'd had to embellish.

Well, lie.

"Vivienne has said some pretty strange things about you, too. . . . " Alexa offered softly. "To everybody. You should know that."

"Really . . . " Rebecca's voice suddenly changed. It was eerie. It wasn't exactly angry. Just very soft, and very icy. "Is that so?"

Bingo. Alexa grinned. "Yes. She says you're a bit of a show-off. And that she doesn't trust you, which is why she wants to act like your friend," she paused. "You know, so that she'd know what was going on with you all the time."

"Well, what do you know?" Rebecca said slowly with that same soft voice. Except now she sounded far away. As if she were lost in thought.

Alexa smiled. What a breeze. "So, now," she began once more, clearing her throat, "want to cancel that shopping date and come with me?"

There was a beat of silence, and then Rebecca began to laugh. "Oh, NO!" she exclaimed loudly. Too loudly. "Especially not now!"

"Wh-what do you mean?" Alexa asked, completely mystified. What was it with Rebecca? Could she do nothing that was black and white, easy to read, an example of logical thinking?

"I mean, I have a plan to just get that little priss Vivienne," Rebecca replied coolly. "That's what."

Alexa couldn't help herself. "Already?"

"Uh-huh," Rebecca replied confidently. "Unfortunately, I have to spend tomorrow afternoon with them. I don't think I can get out of it, but then maybe it's just as well. . . . "

Alexa didn't know whether to laugh or cry. Boy, she was good. Better even than Alexa. One fast mover.

"Well, tell me about the plan!"

"No," Rebecca replied matter-of-factly. "No.

You might give it away without meaning to. Besides, this is my problem. Not yours."

Alexa rolled her eyes. What a joke. Rebecca was the biggest problem, and friend, of course, she'd just about ever had.

Still, why not let Rebecca take the wheel for now?

It was like going on vacation while someone else did the work.

Getting the better of that Crowd was not an easy trick.

"Fine," Alexa finally agreed. "Do I ever get to know the plan?"

"Sure you do," Rebecca laughed. "Meet us all at two o'clock at Gerrards." She paused. "Trust me. Things are going to get pretty nasty!"

"All right!" Alexa exclaimed, one thumb in the air. "Sounds good. Well, I'll see you tomorrow." And a moment later, she hung up the phone.

It was interesting, actually. She'd never met a person who was so like herself. It would have been an unbelievable kick . . . if it wasn't so unnerving.

Leaning back in her chair once more, Alexa smiled broadly at the ceiling. Someone to do her dirty work. Someone else to get that Almost Popular Group.

It was heavenly. Kind of like having an evil assistant.

But a moment later, the smile began to fade.

One thing, though.

As dirty as her work got, Alexa had rules. Things she wouldn't do. Basic things. Serious things. She was, still, sort of, a lady.

But what were Rebecca's rules?

Alexa frowned.

She had no idea what they were.

In fact, she had no idea if her very good friend had any.

14

Priscilla gazed down at her algebra assignment Thursday afternoon.

Amazing. She actually understood it. If not for Ms. Williams' name plastered across the top, she might actually have felt smart again. Confident, too.

She picked up her pencil, glancing up to check the time on the library wall clock. Instead, she suddenly found herself locking stares with Adam Miller.

When had he walked in?

Her heart jumped. She smiled and, then, filled with self-consciousness, looked away. Impulsively, she covered the top of her paper. As if Adam could see it from his seat at the next table.

Seconds later she heard the chair across from hers scraping softly against the floor. She glanced up to find Adam sliding into the seat, a nervous look on his face.

Hurriedly, she folded her assignment sheet

with Ms. Williams' name blazoned across the top in half and placed it in her notebook. If only he would go away and leave her alone. He was too smart for her. What was there to say? She looked down at her algebra textbook and sighed.

If only he would stay.

"You need help?" Adam whispered.

"No," Priscilla shook her head. Great. What was she wearing? A sign that said "I can't keep up"?

"Well, I do," Adam whispered again.

Priscilla looked up at him sharply. "Right," she sniped sarcastically.

"I do . . . " he continued insistently. "I can't write poetry."

Priscilla shrugged. "Me, either." She pretended to look for something in her book bag.

"But you were a great English student last year," Adam continued softly. "I remember."

Priscilla paused. That was true. She was. But so was he.

"Can you help me?" he persisted. "I know I'm smart. But apparently not in everything. In fact . . . "

He didn't finish his sentence.

Priscilla had been looking down at her books. Her bag. Her shoes. Now she lifted her head in response to the silence.

She almost burst out laughing.

Adam Miller, the brain of eighth grade, was

holding up his book report with both hands. A bright red C+ was stamped in the right-hand corner.

"You got that?" she giggled.

"It's not so funny," Adam replied somberly.

Priscilla caught herself immediately. "No," she said quietly. "It really isn't." She paused. "I didn't do much better."

She smiled at Adam. She did, however, feel better.

Ever so slightly.

"Boy," Vivienne breathed, looking around Rebecca's oddly undecorated room. The walls were empty except for a watercolor painting Rebecca had taped to the wall. "We can't wait to meet your father and see his snazzy new office. Also to look in all those new stores in the complex!"

"Is your dad really going to take us out for something to eat afterwards at River's Edge?" Margo chimed in. "My mom says it's a real fancy place!"

"I just want to say that I am thrilled," Rebecca nodded, smiling at everyone. "From the minute I met all of you I just ached to be a part of this!" She paused. "Alexa doesn't hold a candle to you guys."

Priscilla stared at her blankly. Why was she lying like that?

Rebecca looked around the room. "I have tons

of beautiful stuff on order, you know. We just moved in. That's why the room is so drab." She checked her alarm clock. "My dad should be here any minute."

Priscilla leaned back against the wall and looked around. The room was empty all right. But what it really looked like was sad.

"In the meanwhile," Rebecca prattled on, "what should we talk about?"

"Mothers who can't stay out of our business," Margo answered with a big grin. "Mine wanted to know this morning how come I don't wear more royal blue! Does your mom drive you nuts, too?"

"Ummm," Rebecca responded hesitantly, obviously taken a little by surprise. She looked briefly up at the ceiling as if she were trying to decide about something. "I don't exactly have a mother." Then she grinned. As if she'd just announced something that was, on the other hand, delightful. "She kind of moved away when I was very young."

For a moment no one said a word.

"Wow," Vivienne said with uncharacteristic softness. She looked around at her friends as if to say, *You see, she needs us.* "Why?"

"Who cares?" Rebecca replied. "I have a fabulous dad. He'd do anything for me! He gives me lots of freedom and he takes me fabulous places, and he treats me like . . . like . . . a grown-up."

She paused to study her nails. "And he has very neat girlfriends around a lot."

"That's good and bad, I think," Michelle replied. "It must make you feel kind of strange sometimes." She reached over and covered Rebecca's hand with her own.

For the briefest moment, Priscilla saw Rebecca's smile waver. Rebecca's eyes traveled back to the ceiling of her room, stayed there for a few seconds, and then refocused on the group.

Ever so slowly she slid her hand out from under Michelle's.

As if comfort were somehow uncomfortable.

"It's not like that. My dad is great. And if I went like this" — Rebecca snapped her fingers — "he'd come running. I have my ways" — she ran a hand through her hair — "of getting attention." She lifted her chin. "Besides, there's always some weird housekeeper around who does pretty much what I tell her. So . . . "

She smiled big. Too big.

"Sounds good to me," Gina giggled.

There was a beat of silence in the room.

Priscilla looked down at her striped fuchsia-and-purple leggings. Not one girl had asked her yet about the switch in her class. Not one. It had been three whole days. It was as if they'd all just forgotten. It was as if the Rebecca tornado had blown in and taken everything with her . . . and away from Priscilla.

And she'd just watched it happen.

Like a dummy.

"Priscilla, how about you?" Rebecca asked. "Do you get along with your parents?"

Priscilla looked up with surprise. "Y-yes," she stammered.

"They don't get on you about school or anything?" Rebecca pressed on. "Which reminds me, are we all studying together for the next algebra quiz?" She quickly glanced in Priscilla's direction and then down at her nails.

Priscilla could feel the humiliation and sorrow roll over her in a giant wave. Here it was again. The separateness. The thing she was most afraid of.

The them versus her.

The knife in the back. Rebecca-style.

She cleared her throat and looked around the room. Vivienne suddenly started scrounging around in her book bag for probably nothing. Gina apparently found a knot in her hair she just had to get out. Margo started flipping through a notebook, and Michelle was suddenly very intent on the ceiling.

Priscilla couldn't bear it.

They were avoiding her. They had been for three days. They'd never done that before. They were ashamed for her.

Disappointed in her.

It was horrifying.

It was sickening.

And, actually, Priscilla suddenly noticed, it was also infuriating.

She glanced up at Rebecca, who was now smiling at her almost sweetly.

If not tauntingly.

Something inside her suddenly snapped.

She took a deep breath. "Isn't anyone going to ask me straight out why I'm in Ms. Williams' class?" she said fiercely. "Because if you're not, I will." She paused, and in a loud voice she asked, "Priscilla. Why are you in Ms. Williams' class? What happened?"

She looked around the room. Still no one was looking at her. No one but Rebecca, who was still smiling, but with a very odd look of satisfaction on her face.

It was there again. That feeling that Rebecca was after her.

But why?!

"Well, I'll answer the question," Priscilla plowed on. "I'm not perfect! I'm having trouble getting it together this year. I'm not as good a student as I was last year. As you all are. Okay?" Her voice began to waver.

"Of course, it's okay," Gina said quietly. "Don't say that."

"Well, apparently it isn't okay," Priscilla continued, her voice now starting to break. But not out of fear, she suddenly realized.

Out of hurt.

"Otherwise you guys wouldn't have been avoiding this. I mean, I can't believe it's Rebecca who brings it up. Someone I hardly know." Priscilla couldn't seem to stop herself. "Someone hardly any of you know!"

"What's that supposed to mean?" Vivienne retorted sharply.

"Yes, what is that supposed to mean?" Rebecca piped up suddenly. She shot Priscilla a steely look. "This is how you treat a new member?"

"It's how she treats a new member who makes her feel untalented," Vivienne volunteered loudly.

Priscilla sucked in her breath with horror.

"VIVIENNE!" Michelle cried out. "That's a terrible thing to say. We don't know Rebecca super-well. You know that." She turned to Rebecca. "In this club we try not to put each other down, but some of us forget that." She shot Vivienne an annoyed look. Then she turned to Priscilla. "To tell you the truth, we didn't bring it up, Priscilla, because we thought you didn't want to talk about it!"

Priscilla hesitated. Why didn't she believe that?

That wasn't the Crowd way at all. They helped each other talk. Get things out.

On the other hand, Priscilla thought to herself bitterly, that was before Rebecca.

"Yeah. You snuck into Ms. Williams' class, and

so we figured that's how you wanted to handle it,"
Margo added. She tilted her head to one side. "We
haven't forgotten about you at all." She reached
over and squeezed Priscilla's hand. "You're our
Priscilla," she added affectionately.

Priscilla nodded. She was also, according to
them, their jealous blob.

"Besides, Priscilla, just because Rebecca can
draw doesn't mean you can't," Gina added softly.

Priscilla nodded unhappily and then looked
around the circle. Her eyes rested on Rebecca.

Why was she gunning for Priscilla's spot? Why
couldn't she just go away!?

Suddenly the front door slammed, a woman's
laugh rang through the air, and seconds later a
very handsome man with thick brown curly hair,
wearing tight jeans, a workshirt, spectacular cow-
boy boots, and a blazer, stood in the doorway to
Rebecca's room.

"Becca Tecca!" he called out cheerfully. "How's
my girl?"

Rebecca smiled almost shyly, and then looked
down at the floor. "Fine, Paul," she said quietly.

"A little more enthusiasm for your dad, please!"
he joked.

"This is your dad?" Vivienne blurted out, and,
then, turning beet-red, she covered her face with
her hands.

"I'm it!" Mr. Lake assured her. "But you can

call me Paul. And this" — he disappeared, returning seconds later with a woman in tow — "is Liz. Say hi, Liz!"

"Hi!" the woman obeyed. "What's up, girls?"

Priscilla could not believe her eyes. Liz was possibly the sexiest person she'd ever seen. Her navy Lycra skirt was very short, revealing very pretty legs. Her blue-and-white-striped sweater was very tight, revealing a very large chest, and her bushy, stylish reddish-brown hair seemed cut for the sole purpose of showing off her gorgeous, green, almond-shaped eyes.

"We just stopped by to pick up a tie," Paul Lake said. "Don't let us interrupt. We'll be out of your way in no time."

"Wh-what do you mean?" Rebecca stammered. "We're supposed to be going with you today. . . . "

"Oh, man," Mr. Lake shook his head with a grimace. He paused for a long moment. "I'm impossible. You're right. But I can't take you. I'm sorry, hon. Liz and I have something to do. . . . "

"B-but . . . everyone's here," Rebecca protested with uncharacteristic distress. "Can't you . . . "

"No, I can't." Mr. Lake's expression suddenly grew sullen. "Look, Becca, you're a big girl." He glanced around the room at the other girls. "You all are," he added, his voice dripping with false flattery. Suddenly he shoved his hand in his pocket, pulled out a wallet, and threw a fifty-dollar bill into his daughter's lap. "Take everyone out for dinner," he offered, smiling broadly.

"We'll just eat at home," Vivienne piped up. "That's okay."

"Well then, Becca, I guess it's time for a new sweater for you? Huh?" Mr. Lake chuckled. "We'll go to my office another time."

"Yeah," Rebecca replied stonily.

"Yessiree. Just what I like. A happy kid," Mr. Lake responded almost coldly. "Ms. Maple is in the kitchen. She'll make you whatever you want for supper." Then he turned to Liz. "Shall we?" he asked. Liz giggled, waved to the girls, and the two of them disappeared down the hall.

For a moment, the room was very quiet.

"It doesn't matter," Michelle said matter-of-factly. "What's so great about an office?" She paused. "Your father's real handsome," she added.

Rebecca nodded. "Uh-huh."

"He's so young!" Vivienne exclaimed.

"Can you imagine having HIM as a father?" Gina giggled.

Priscilla closed her eyes for a brief moment. No. Actually, she couldn't. Not one who looked like guys from her class except a little older. Not one who wanted to be called by his first name as if he were a buddy.

And certainly not one who dated a woman who

127

looked like that, and who changed plans on his daughter as easily as flipping on and off a light.

Priscilla envisioned her own father.

Suddenly, having a college professor who looked like one and acted like one seemed real nice.

Suddenly she almost pitied Rebecca. But not quite.

Actually, she didn't know what she felt. Or why.

She just needed to get away for a moment. Pull herself together. "Where's the bathroom?" she asked.

"At the end of the hall, next to my father's office," Rebecca replied. A second later, she smiled sweetly. "We won't do anything without you."

Priscilla nodded, stood up stiffly, and walked out of the room. She could feel the rage surging within her. "We?" How had Rebecca wormed her way in so fast? So snugly? So completely?

Stomping down the hall, Priscilla glanced to her left into Mr. Lake's office and was about to step past it when something caught her eye.

A large, light-brown box. On it were marked the words PROMOTION GIFT FOR ROSE-LAND USA.

Priscilla sucked in her breath.

Cascading from the box in every color imaginable were men's neckties decorated with the identical, machine-stamped, long-winding rosebud that adorned the ties of The Practically Popular Crowd.

Priscilla moved quietly into the room and considered, for a long moment, dragging the box into the meeting.

Exposing the lies.

Putting an end to Ms. Rebecca Lake for good.

But seconds later, she opted against it.

Rebecca would think of something. She'd cry. She'd insist the rosebud was her design. She'd flatter them with her desire to be included. She'd insist Priscilla was jealous.

And in the end, the Crowd would embrace her.

Because Rebecca was a talented, glittering fake.

And what was she? Nothing but the real, if not too smart, thing. That's what.

Angrily, Priscilla turned to walk out of the room.

Where were her loyal friends? The ones who cared about her? Believed in her?

She leaned against the doorjamb.

They were nowhere.

In fact, they deserved to be dumped. Left to survive Rebecca on their own. Priscilla smiled bitterly. It was a terrific thought.

Revenge had its pluses.

Rebecca would make every single one of them miserable. And soon, too.

She could smell it coming.

Of course, revenge on each other was not the
Practically Popular Crowd way.

Which brought to light a very burning question.

Was she really, truly, deeply, still a member?

Priscilla Levitt honestly didn't know.

Or, was it, care?

15

Alexa took one look at Rebecca standing outside of Gerrards and decided everything
would be fine. Her funny little inkling of trouble
to come was, well, unfair.

She studied Rebecca from across the street. She
looked great. Actually, beautiful. Her tight blue
jeans with the holes at the knees showed off her
slim long legs, and the scoop-necked black pullover set off her dark hair to perfection.

And, really, all she was doing was standing
there. Holding a large denim tote bag stuffed with
paper bags. She had, it seemed, already started
shopping.

Alexa smiled as she crossed the street.

"Hi!" Rebecca called out eagerly as Alexa approached. She began walking toward Alexa. "You
look great today!"

Alexa smiled and nodded. She did look pretty
good. Her black denim jeans were a perfect fit,
and the pink, long-sleeved, boat-necked Tee

showed off her chest perfectly. That was something she certainly had over Rebecca. A B cup.

Still, what did Rebecca mean by "today"? Alexa looked pretty good every day. Didn't she?

"So," Rebecca smiled with an odd gleam in her eye. "Are we ready?" Suddenly she reached into her denim tote and pulled out a smaller faded one. She handed it to Alexa. "Here. I thought you might like this to shop with. You know how those paper ones always break." She plucked a paper bag from her own bag and placed it in Alexa's. "Empty bags look so lonely, don't you think?" she asked with a giggle.

Alexa hesitated. "I guess so," she said slowly. "Ummm, Rebecca. How about telling me now what you've got in store for Vivienne?" She looked down at the bag. What a weird gesture.

"Uh-uh." Rebecca shook her head mischievously. "This is my show. I want you to enjoy it. . . . "

"I don't like surprises," Alexa forced a chuckle from somewhere inside her. It wasn't easy. That bad feeling was coming back again. "Come on," she went for a smile. It didn't happen. "Tell me . . . "

"No," Rebecca responded bluntly. "You'll find out soon enough."

Alexa sighed.

Somehow, she wasn't so sure.

Somehow, she had the oddest feeling that when she did find out, it would be way too late. . . .

"Hello, everyone!" Priscilla called out with false gaiety at noon sharp. The Crowd was already there, each wearing their Rebecca ties, waiting for her outside of Gerrards. "I'm not late, am I?"

Priscilla glanced at Vivienne's tie with bitterness. It didn't say "We're a Crowd." It said "We're Rebecca's Crowd." Didn't they see?

"You're fine," Michelle answered with a big smile. "Come on. Let's go in and see if Rebecca's here yet." Priscilla nodded. It was amazing — just the sound of Rebecca's name made her blood boil. She watched as all her friends moved enthusiastically through the big glass doors, anxious to find their new Crowd member.

It was positively depressing.

Priscilla moved toward the doors as if she were slogging through mud. Everything was so different. They used to be such a cozy group. But now there was a stranger in their midst, and no one seemed to see the trouble that was coming. Except for her.

It was such a lonely feeling.

Such a bad feeling.

She resented it like crazy.

"Oh, there she is!" Vivienne called out merrily. "Rebecca, over here. We're . . . "

Suddenly, she stopped talking.

Priscilla glanced to her right to see all four girls lined up, perfectly still, as if they'd turned to stone, staring down the center aisle of the store.

Priscilla turned to follow their stare.

For a moment, she, too, was stunned.

Rebecca Lake was standing by the makeup counter, waving them over with none other than Alexa Craft by her side. "Join us!" she called out. "Come on!"

"What's Alexa doing here?" Margo practically hissed.

"Maybe they just ran into each other," Michelle whispered as she took a tentative step forward.

"Yes. That must be it. . . . " Vivienne mumbled unhappily.

Priscilla swallowed hard. It was starting. No question. Rebecca knew this was an insult. She had to. But she didn't seem to care.

"What's everyone waiting for?" Rebecca insisted loudly. "Let's go! I'm off to the belts and bags." And with that, she turned quickly around and began heading toward the accessories department, Alexa close behind.

Followed by everyone else.

With a sigh of relief, Alexa trailed energetically after Rebecca.

That hadn't been bad at all.

Hardly a retaliation, by Alexa's standards.

And here she'd thought Rebecca was going to really cause trouble. Do something absolutely . . . dastardly.

And all it was, was a little confrontation. A little personal statement. A "See, I'm not just your friend at all" kind of performance.

It was almost disappointing. She'd seen that hurt look on Vivienne's face many times before. Big deal.

"So," Alexa began, slipping her arm through Rebecca's. This was no one to be afraid of. Not at all. "That sure showed Vivienne, huh?" No point making Rebecca feel small or unimaginative.

It was a nice little plan. Certainly Viv was embarrassed.

"What?" Rebecca asked as she fingered a woven leather deep green belt with gold trim. "What showed her?"

"Well," Alexa replied, running her fingers over a purple suede thin belt, "us. Planning to meet her and her friends, but showing up here with me. . . . "

"Oh!" Rebecca chuckled. "Alexa. That wasn't my plan. That was just, well, a bonus." She chuckled some more. "I mean, give me some credit. Okay?"

Alexa sucked in her breath. Actually, no. It wasn't okay.

"Yeah, sure . . . " she stammered. That awful feeling was returning now. She could feel it tightening its grasp.

Alexa pretended extreme interest in a silver-and-turquoise chain belt. "I sure wish I knew what you were up to," she continued slowly. Cautiously. "I told you, I hate surprises. . . . "

Rebecca turned toward Alexa and rested one hand on her shoulder. "Alexa, you're going to thank me when this is over." She reached over and picked up the silver belt Alexa had been admiring.

Then she glanced down the aisle. "Oh, look. Here they come," Rebecca whispered gleefully. Alexa turned to see Vivienne, Michelle, Margo, Gina, and Priscilla walking slowly toward them.

It looked like a funeral procession.

Which, in a way, was rather funny.

She turned back to Rebecca. "Well, they look happy," she giggled.

"Trust me," Rebecca whispered. "By the time they leave this store, that will look like they're partying." Then she plucked the green braided leather belt from its hook, wrapped it around her hand so that it formed a neat small coil, and plunked it casually, quickly, and secretively into her tote.

Alexa stared at her wide-eyed. "What are you

doing?" she whispered, louder than she'd intended.

An impossible thought had just crossed her mind. Ridiculous, really. Paranoid, in fact.

Rebecca nodded in the direction of Alexa's tote. "Don't look now. But nothing you wouldn't do, too" — she paused — "Comrade."

Then, as if she were nothing but a bubble, Rebecca seemed to simply float from the counter and back toward the Crowd.

Alexa looked down into her tote. She gasped.

Nestled at the bottom of the dull blue bag, almost hidden by the paper bag, was the silver-and-turquoise belt she'd been admiring only moments earlier.

Alexa stood rooted to the spot.

She turned to watch with disbelief as Rebecca warmly greeted The Practically Something Crowd.

She stood and watched as the six of them exchanged pleasantries, kissed, and discussed just how much fun they were about to have.

But, most of all, she stood in awe of a very simple fact.

Rebecca was shoplifting.

And if she didn't take a stand real soon, no matter what the consequences, no matter how much time she'd have wasted winning Rebecca over . . . she would be shoplifting, too.

Alexa closed her eyes and tried to think.

She waited for the strength she knew she had, somewhere, to surface.

The choice, Alexa knew, was crystal clear.

But so was something else.

Somehow, she couldn't make it.

16

Priscilla was positive she'd seen it wrong.

It was just too outrageous.

She turned to look at her friends. No one looked surprised, or shocked, or even slightly perplexed.

No one had seemed to see it. Or at least the same way she had.

But, then, what else was new?

"I guess you just kind of ran into Alexa here?" Vivienne was saying sweetly. Hopefully. Naively.

"Yes," Rebecca replied quickly. "Of course. You don't think I'd have arranged this?"

"Of course not!" Margo laughed. "Goodness, that would really make you a nut, now wouldn't it?"

Rebecca laughed. Too loudly, Priscilla thought. "Yes. It really would!"

"I say we head over to the junior department," Rebecca announced. She bowed her head down as if she were about to tell a secret. "Listen, let's just let Alexa come along. I don't know. She looks kind of lonely."

The group was silent for a moment.

"That's okay with me," Michelle responded unenthusiastically, "but I'm not asking her."

"Fine, I will," Rebecca volunteered quickly. She turned and called out to Alexa. "Come. You, too. Let's all go!" she sang out cheerfully, and then, as if she were the Pied Piper, she began to lead the way toward the escalator, the big denim bag swinging beside her.

Alexa scooted up the escalator, shoved Michelle ever so slightly aside, and took up a spot directly beside Rebecca, who was now standing in front of everyone with a broad smile planted on her face.

"I don't like this," Alexa muttered anxiously.

"Don't be silly," Rebecca shook her head. "Don't be immature."

Alexa turned away, startled. No one spoke to her that way. Ever. Well, except Rebecca.

"You won't get caught," Rebecca hurried on. "Trust me."

"How do you know?" Alexa replied curtly, not at all sure that was the point, anyway. "I am not immature," she added irritably.

"Because the belts don't have those tags on them that set the alarm off when you go through the door."

Alexa stole a glance into the tote. That was true. But, somehow, it didn't matter.

She glanced sideways at Rebecca. "I might put this belt back before we leave the store," she whispered. "I don't really want it anyway."

Rebecca gave her a skeptical look. "Yes, you do."

They were reaching the second floor, and Rebecca stepped off the escalator, Alexa a half-beat behind her. "You're just scared. Calm down. This can be fun." She paused. "And it will cement our friendship. It'll be our secret. . . . " She flashed Alexa a big, almost challenging, smile. "Isn't that neat?"

Alexa shrugged. "Yeah," she murmured. "Real neat."

"I need a pair of jeans," Michelle called out as she headed for the denim wear.

"I'm looking for a long black top to go over my black leggings," Margo muttered. "Boy, I wish I could get away with a short one."

"Maybe you can," Gina assured her. "Come, let's look. You have to stop seeing yourself like that."

Priscilla watched as the girls separated in the junior department. Vivienne with Michelle, Margo with Gina, and Rebecca off on her own.

Priscilla began to trail her.

Rebecca stopped at a silky tank top and ran her fingers admiringly over the soft, supple material. Then she passed it by.

Priscilla feigned interest in a short black skirt, holding it up to herself in the mirror as she watched Rebecca pull out a cherry-red, long-sleeved top and hold it out in front of her.

Once again, Rebecca returned the item to the rack.

Priscilla frowned.

And then, suddenly, though it happened so quickly she could barely believe it, Rebecca made her move.

Reaching out toward a pair of floral Lycra tights, Rebecca grabbed it from the single rack resting next to matching tops and threw one, and then another, into her tote.

Seconds later she was across the aisle, once again studying the same silky tank top she'd been looking at before.

Priscilla stood frozen to the spot.

There was a movement from a few feet to her left. She turned to see a salesgirl, who had clearly, by the expression on her face, spotted Rebecca.

Priscilla stepped back. She averted her eyes.

She waited for the salesgirl to pounce.

But, to her incredible surprise, nothing happened.

Suddenly, she remembered why.

Rebecca hadn't tried to leave the store with the

items. Not yet, anyway. A salesperson, she had read somewhere, could prove nothing unless a shoplifter tried to leave without paying.

Priscilla took a deep breath and let it out slowly.

And, hadn't she also read, that anyone accompanying the shoplifter could get in trouble as well?

Priscilla whirled around to locate her friends. They were in the pants aisle. She could hear Vivienne over at the jackets. Gina at the sweaters.

If she didn't do something, each one of her dearest friends in the world would find themselves in the most unfair, embarrassing, and horrendous situation she could think of.

She pursed her lips.

Of course, in a way, they deserved it.

Unlike herself.

There was a way out, too. But only for her. Priscilla could hardly believe she was thinking it. She pushed the thought away.

Seconds later, Priscilla could feel the tears welling up.

But if she did speak up, there was no telling what Rebecca would say. Or do. And whether Priscilla would survive it. A tear began to make its way down her cheek.

Why did she have to be so perceptive? Why did she have to know all along there was something dead wrong?

Why did she have to feel so powerless, just when she needed all the strength in the world?

17

Alexa stood across the aisle from Vivienne, glaring as she watched her former closest friend sift through the sale rack.

Darn her. If it hadn't been for Vivienne, she probably wouldn't be standing here, squirming desperately, like a bug in a spiderweb.

She pretended to study a navy-blue blazer. It was hardly her style. Still, it gave her something to do while she fought the rage. For a split second, Alexa considered ripping off the neat row of glistening gold buttons. One by one.

Just to make herself feel better.

"Are you sure?" She suddenly heard Vivienne's voice above the steady beat of rock music.

Whirling around, Alexa watched as Rebecca held up a deep v-necked, bright-red, slim-cut minidress, designed for someone with a very curvy figure. It looked about as right for Vivienne as an Indian headdress.

"Absolutely," Rebecca responded in a tone as

sweet as honey. She put the hanger in Vivienne's hand and gave her a gentle push toward the dressing rooms. "You'll look great. Don't come out without it on. I have to see . . . "

Quickly, excitedly, Vivienne made her way across the floor. Alexa shook her head. She was going to look like a fool.

Suddenly, she stopped. Maybe that was it? Rebecca was going to make Vivienne look idiotic? She turned to study Rebecca, who was now smiling smugly.

Yes. That must be it. It was certainly mean.

Alexa frowned. But it hardly compared to the way she'd made Alexa feel.

Like a trapped, low-down criminal.

Filled with anger, she practically stamped her way over to Rebecca. Take it easy, a voice inside her head instructed. You've come this far. Be smart. You can find a way out of this. You can make the right girl pay.

"Can I talk to you, Rebecca, please?" she whispered, though it came out more like a hiss.

"Why, sure," Rebecca responded sweetly. She eyed Alexa with just a touch of amusement. "Goodness, you look very upset."

"I . . . I am," Alexa practically sputtered. "I came with you today because you said you were going to get Vivienne, and instead you stick her in a ridiculous dress and I'm walking around feeling . . . "

"Shame on you . . . " Rebecca whispered. "You missed the big payback, Alexa." She smiled. "It's all in place. I'm surprised at you. That dress is just a little fun I'm having."

Alexa looked at her in bewilderment. "The big payback?"

Rebecca nodded. "I really shouldn't tell you this, but I mean, well, I've outdone myself. I can't hold it in." Grabbing Alexa's arm, she dragged her into a corner next to a rack of down coats.

"I threw a little something into one of Vivienne's deep jacket pockets, if you know what I mean."

Alexa shook her head in exasperation.

"I mean I put a little shoulder bag in her jacket pocket. Tag on. All systems ready to go."

Alexa nodded, as if she were getting it. Which she wasn't. Not at all. "What did she say?" Alexa asked, completely confused now. "Vivienne agreed to shoplift?"

"Alexa!" Rebecca started laughing loudly now. "Wake up! Would you? I thought you were a pro at this kind of thing!" Then she lowered her voice. "Ms. Viv doesn't know. That's the beauty of the thing. She'll walk out of the store, the bells will start ringing, and . . . " — she held up her hands — "as only Viv would say, '*Voilà!*' "

"Ah . . . " Alexa nodded.

So there it was.

The plan she'd been waiting for.

She tried to smile.

It certainly was awful. Rebecca sure meant business.

Yessiree.

Good ol' Viv had finally gone too far.

Alexa could feel herself continuing to nod, as if she completely agreed . . . while her thoughts sped wildly, frantically, in other directions. . . .

This was all wrong. Being here. Rebecca. Shoplifting. Looking for friendship with a person she didn't even know. Or like. Or understand. Or want to know.

A person she was actually afraid of.

It was all wrong.

And she had to get out.

"It's not so funny. . . . " Alexa blurted out faintly, looking down at her white high-top sneakers. The nodding had stopped.

"Excuse me?" Rebecca replied in a tone Alexa had never quite heard before. It was almost . . . chilling.

She looked up and into Rebecca's steel-gray eyes.

"I said . . . " Alexa cleared her throat nervously. "I think I'm going to put this belt back" — she pointed to her bag — "and leave. This whole thing is not me." She attempted a friendly smile. No point completely alienating Rebecca. She still had power over lots of kids, and who knew what she would do if . . .

"No, I don't understand," Rebecca replied icily.

147

"Or, rather, I do understand one thing." She paused for effect. "You are a wimp."

Alexa stared at her blankly, mouth slightly open for a few seconds. Nothing was worth this. No person. No crowd. No future fights for the popularity crown. NOTHING.

"Listen, Rebecca," Alexa began, the anger welling up in her like an overdue volcano, "you are a terrible, dishonest, backbiting, two-timing person. You don't care about anyone but yourself. I don't need you."

Rebecca smiled with unnerving serenity. "Oh, Alexa, that reminds me." Her voice was so low, it was almost difficult to hear. "I must have forgotten to tell you . . . you really ought to wear more blue. Did you know that's Mac's favorite color? He told me when he asked me out for a soda yesterday." She patted Alexa's shoulder. "He's really a bore. Maybe if you wore something blue, he'd stop chasing me. . . . "

And with that, Rebecca turned on her heels and walked swiftly down the aisle, disappearing behind a rack of tops.

Alexa stood rooted to the spot.

"Well!" Vivienne's voice suddenly rang through the air. "*Voilà!*"

Alexa turned around to see Vivienne pivoting slowly in the center of the department while her friends, minus Rebecca, stared gape-mouthed at the disheartening sight.

"What do you think?" Vivienne asked hopefully, a tentative smile playing across her lips, one hand self-consciously pulling the tip of the deep V up two inches, while the rest of the dress sagged unattractively upon her slim, straight frame.

A deafening silence followed the question.

Alexa looked quickly away and leaned, sickened, against the wall.

She had a choice. Vivienne was about to get arrested, and it was up to her to stop it. Sure, they'd done some ugly things to each other. But this was different. This was serious.

Really serious.

She had to tell Viv. She had to take a stand.

Stepping out from the racks, Alexa was about to walk over to Vivienne when Rebecca's voice cut through the air.

"Vivienne, I'm not sure that's quite right." Rebecca spoke tenderly. Gently. She held up a deep green scoop-necked dress with an empire waist and walked swiftly to Vivienne's side. "This might do better."

"Yes!" Michelle cried out with evident relief.

"Absolutely," Margo enthused. She smiled at Rebecca. "What a great eye you have!"

Vivienne reached out to Rebecca and gave her a hug. "You are the best thing that ever happened to Port Andrews," she gushed.

Alexa stopped dead in her tracks.

Oh, please.

These were the people she had to protect?

Never mind.

What was she? A policeman? Vivienne's fairy godmother? She had no obligations to anyone. Least of all Ms. Bennis.

No. Vivienne deserved it.

They all deserved it. That whole pathetic crowd. They were blind, and stupid, and if it weren't for them, she wouldn't even be here. If they hadn't made such a fuss over Rebecca, probably no one else would have, either. Alexa would have still been number one. No competition. No threats. No problems.

No. If she was going to lose her status to Rebecca Lake, they all deserved something at least as bad. . . .

At least as embarrassing, and unfair, and . . . cruel.

Alexa Craft turned on her heels and, with the turquoise belt clearly in hand, headed for the escalator.

Going down, she thought.

And then she grimaced.

In more ways than one.

18

Priscilla watched silently as Vivienne Bennis, the smartest girl in eighth grade, made her way back to the dressing room in the ridiculous red dress.

She watched as Alexa's blonde head disappeared on the down escalator after what had clearly been an argument with Rebecca.

And she watched as Rebecca calmly and serenely continued her charade as the latest, greatest member of The Practically Popular Crowd.

"Priscilla!" Margo called out. "What are you doing over there by your lonesome? Come on over!"

Priscilla smiled and began the short walk to the tight little circle that had already formed in the center of the department.

"Hi, stranger!" Rebecca said merrily. She reached out and flicked a strand of Priscilla's hair out of her eyes. "Such great thick hair you have!" she exclaimed.

Priscilla almost cringed. She checked her watch. They would be leaving the store soon. Her stomach was starting to ache.

She wanted to leave. Desperately. Just get away. The choice she hadn't wanted to think about earlier was pushing its way into her consciousness, tempting her fiercely.

"Go on," it was saying. "Do it."

Priscilla tried to ignore it. She couldn't.

She began to consider the possibility.

She could take care of herself. She could make up an excuse and leave early.

Simply avoid everything altogether. Let the Crowd find out on their own, while she just walked off. Free and clear.

It would serve them right for doubting her. Suspecting her. Letting a stranger into their circle without her REAL approval.

Besides, would they ever believe her once Rebecca was through denying it? Squirming out of it somehow.

Priscilla glanced around the circle.

Probably not.

They were chatting with each other so happily. So confidently. So sure of themselves.

So like how she used to feel. It was enraging.

It was sickening.

It was time to leave.

She took a step backwards.

Suddenly Gina reached out and touched her

hand. "Are you okay, Pris? You look funny," she whispered.

Priscilla nodded and suddenly found herself smiling back.

Being drawn into the warmth, the friendship.

It was automatic. Natural. Even sincere.

And in that instant, she knew.

She could never betray them. Not Gina, or Michelle, or Margo, and no, not even Vivienne. Not in a million years . . .

She whirled around to face Rebecca.

If she was going to do it, it might as well be now. Before she chickened out. If she lost, so be it.

"Please put everything back, Rebecca. . . ." Priscilla said slowly and deliberately. "Please. Don't get us all in trouble."

"What are you talking about?" Rebecca laughed.

For a moment, Priscilla was startled. Rebecca sounded genuinely perplexed.

"Yes, what are you talking about?" Margo laughed.

"What's she talking about?" Gina asked, glancing from Rebecca to Michelle nervously.

"I mean the items she's been shoving in her tote," Priscilla answered as calmly as she could. Her voice was beginning to break. "Hidden between the packages."

Rebecca gave Priscilla a long, thoughtful look.

Then she smiled.

And then she reached into her tote and did precisely what Priscilla had hoped against hope she wouldn't do.

"You mean this stuff?" she asked. She pulled out the stockings and belt. "Why should I put them back? I'm going to buy them."

She looked at Priscilla wide-eyed.

Priscilla could feel herself faltering in her resolve. In her convictions. In her absolute knowledge that Rebecca was lying.

"You . . . you . . . know why," she managed, desperately trying to stay strong. Trust her own instincts. What was it about Rebecca? Why was she always crumbling around her? How could she blame her Crowd for buckling, when even she, knowing what she knew, was already distrusting herself?

"I do?" Rebecca said slowly, looking at the items in her hand as if they held the secret, the key to the mystery only Priscilla seemed to know about. She stood that way for a long moment and then suddenly she started to laugh. "Oh. No!" she started to giggle. "Priscilla, I can't believe you would stoop this low!" She looked around at the other girls, pointing a finger at Priscilla. "I do believe she thinks I'm shoplifting!"

"YOU'RE WHAT!" Vivienne's voice seemed to bounce off the walls. She descended on the group like a lioness, defending her cub. "PRISCILLA! YOU DON'T?!"

Priscilla stood stiffly in her place. It was true. She did. Pretty much, anyway. In fact, it was absolutely true, a moment ago. But now? She began chewing on her lower lip. Rebecca seemed so sure. So outraged.

So innocent.

"Priscilla," Gina said softly, pulling at her arm. "Why don't you just apologize. Okay?"

Priscilla looked at her friend dumbfounded.

No, it wasn't okay. But what choice did she have?

She had no proof. She just had her instinct.

And in this Crowd, that didn't seem to count for much. Not anymore, anyway.

Priscilla shrugged.

"Priscilla Levitt, you have to apologize," Vivienne said venomously, both hands on her hips. "You have gone too far. You really have."

Priscilla turned her eyes to Rebecca, who was smiling at her softly, waiting, it seemed, with infinite patience.

"I'm sorry," Priscilla finally whispered. Tightly. Curtly. There was no way out.

Rebecca was winning this battle. As she did all battles. Priscilla turned her back and feigned interest in a black sweater. If she could just go home.

Now.

The hate was beginning to overwhelm her.

Shock her.

Spill from Rebecca onto every member of the Crowd.

Even onto herself . . .

"Well, I'd say I've about had it with shopping around," Margo volunteered a little too brightly. "Anyone want to go?"

"Me," Gina responded quickly.

"I do, too," Michelle agreed, nervously twisting her hair.

"Should I get this dress?" Viv asked as she pivoted in front of a mirror.

"Yes," Margo declared. "And then let's all go."

Priscilla watched as Vivienne sprinted toward the dressing room, then she took a deep breath and turned around. "Yes. Let's."

"Actually, I'm not through here," Rebecca suddenly interjected. "You guys go on ahead. I think I'll just do a bit more looking around." She tapped Priscilla on the shoulder. "You look so worried! No hard feelings!"

Priscilla nodded. As if she hoped that was true. As if she were relieved. As if she cared. All the while feeling like the doomed heroine in a sci-fi movie. Like the only person who saw an alien spaceship land, or a peapod turn into a person, or a giant ant.

She began making her way down the aisle, from

red sweaters to blue and red vests, to white blouses and green Tees. One by one she moved the hangers aside as if she were looking for a particular style, or size, or material.

But she wasn't. She was looking for herself. For her center. For the part of her that trusted in what she saw. In what she knew. In what she felt . . .

"Ready," Vivienne called out from the cash register. "I'm all packed up." She started heading toward the escalator.

"Bye, Rebecca," Vivienne called out anxiously before she got on. "You're okay about all this, aren't you?" She nodded toward Priscilla.

"Oh, yes," Rebecca waved away her concern. "Bye!"

"Bye!" Margo, Michelle, and Gina called out in unison as they stepped onto the escalator and began to descend.

Priscilla stood silently on the moving steps, feeling as if she were sinking into a bottomless pit. She'd saved everyone today. She was almost sure of that. But she couldn't keep it up. She didn't even want to. No one appreciated it. No one wanted it.

The thing was, did she dare give up? Something else was coming. Something terrible . . .

Slowly she followed the girls as they made their way toward the front doors. And yet what could she prove? Suspicions. Machine-made ties. Items stuffed into shopping bags. Phony compliments. Insensitive remarks and gestures . . . mostly directed at her. She stopped for the briefest moment to admire a multicolored Peruvian wrap belt. It didn't add up to anything that bad.

Nothing she could point to and say, "You see! Keep away from her! I'm not just jealous! I'm scared!"

She turned just as Vivienne began to walk through the doorway onto the street. How was it the smartest girl in the world had noticed so little? Could be swayed so much? Was it actually possible that Priscilla was simply wrong?

And, then, an instant later, it happened.

A blaring two-tone alarm suddenly resounded through the store. A maddening red light above the exit door began to flash brightly. Accusingly. And under it, Vivienne, with both arms wrapped around herself in a useless attempt at self-protection, stood wide-eyed and petrified.

The security staff were upon the Practically Popular Crowd in seconds.

19

"Excuse me," a tall, not unkind-looking man in a blue uniform said as he slipped his hand firmly around Vivienne's arm. "Would you and your friends please step aside?"

"I didn't do anything. . . . " Vivienne protested with uncharacteristic meekness. She turned toward her friends, a look of panic etched on her face. Vivienne's eyes settled on Priscilla. They were begging for help.

For a moment Priscilla stood perfectly still, stunned by her neediness.

Then, suddenly, she squared her shoulders and moved a step closer to the security man. Something inside her was moving. Shifting.

Triumphantly returning.

"Excuse me, but could you tell us what's going on?" She reached out and placed a hand protectively on Vivienne's shoulder. "She wouldn't do anything wrong."

The man smiled. "Well, maybe, but it's my job

to be sure. Frankly, I heard a group of girls might be shoplifting."

"Oh, you have that wrong," Vivienne began talking very quickly as he gently took the shopping bag from her hand and looked inside, checking the receipt. "Priscilla here thought a friend of ours was shoplifting and someone must have overheard us." She shot Priscilla an angry look.

Priscilla stood her ground. Vivienne would know the truth soon enough.

"Hmmm," the security man commented. "The ticket's been properly removed from the dress." He stood back and studied Vivienne.

His eyes fell on the deep outside patch pockets of her kelly-green jacket. Grimly he put his hand out. "Miss, I'm sorry, but I'm going to have to check your jacket. Would you take it off, please?"

Clearly humiliated, Vivienne averted her eyes as she self-consciously removed her blazer. "Here. You'll see. There's nothing," she muttered as she handed it over.

The man felt around in the right pocket, shrugged, and moved to the left. Suddenly he stopped, and with a mixture of reluctance and satisfaction on his face, the security man pulled out a slim red leather shoulder bag. "This," he said sadly, "isn't nothing."

"HOW DID THAT GET THERE?!" Vivienne cried out, whirling around to look at her friends. "WHO WOULD HAVE DONE SOMETHING

LIKE THIS?" Her eyes traveled in disbelief from Margo to Michelle to Gina and to Priscilla, a hurt, confused expression on her face. Finally, and with obvious pain, she turned toward the escalator and looked up toward the second floor.

A moment later Vivienne's eyes, brimming with tears, sought out Priscilla's. "Rebecca?" Vivienne whimpered.

"I'm afraid I'm going to have to check all your jackets," the security man said, holding out his hand. One by one the girls allowed him to check their pockets.

He found nothing else.

"Well, girls, what are we going to do about this?"

Priscilla stepped forward immediately. "I can straighten this out. Can we please all go upstairs?"

"Well, I don't know. Why?" he answered matter-of-factly.

"Because the person who is responsible for this trick is upstairs," Priscilla replied evenly. Then she smiled. Broadly. For the first time in a very long time, she actually felt happy. It was the oddest feeling. Here she was about to get arrested. And she couldn't remember feeling this good. Ever.

Single file they all solemnly boarded the escalator to the second floor. Priscilla closed her eyes. She wasn't exactly clear how she was going to handle this. What she would say. How she would say it. She looked anxiously back at the security man. Or if he would listen. Make the right decision.

Let her and her friends go.

Priscilla's hand gripped the escalator handrail tightly. Her friends were depending on her. Trusting her to set things straight. It was a very difficult feeling. A gentle smile began to play across her lips.

But a good and familiar one, too.

Priscilla hadn't taken two steps off the escalator when she spotted Rebecca. She was standing in the aisle between the down coats and wool jackets. Actually, she was stooping quite a bit.

Rebecca, Priscilla realized instantly, was actually trying to hide. It was an infuriating thought, and without a moment's hesitation, she stomped angrily toward her.

By the time Rebecca realized she'd been spotted, every member of The Practically Popular Crowd was a few feet away.

Priscilla grabbed her arm and pulled her out into the open space. "How could you?" she hissed.

"Not this again," Rebecca tried, her eyes flitting nervously from girl to girl. "I thought we straightened . . . "

"I TRUSTED YOU!" Vivienne cried out, her slim body trembling with hurt and rage. "How could you do this?" Her voice tapered off into a dull whisper.

"Do what?!" Rebecca giggled. "Vivienne, I don't know what . . . "

"STOP IT!" Priscilla practically bellowed. "TELL HIM WHAT YOU DID! TELL HIM YOU PLANTED THAT BAG ON VIVIENNE. TELL HIM NOW!"

Rebecca's confident smile suddenly began to disappear. "You can't prove a thing," she said quietly. "Nothing."

"Well, someone put that bag in Vivienne's pocket," Michelle snapped. "And it wasn't us."

Rebecca shook her head and looked around the circle of girls. "Did it ever occur to you that maybe Vivienne did it. That maybe she's a liar?" Rebecca glanced at the security man. "Can you believe they're trying to pin this on me?"

"I did see you placing items in your bag," an unfamiliar voice piped up from behind them. Priscilla whirled around to see the salesgirl she had spotted earlier, watching Rebecca.

"You're calling me a liar? After everything I've done for you?" Vivienne suddenly cried out as if she'd completely missed the last exchange. "A LIAR?"

Rebecca whirled around to face her. "You bet I am! You think you're such an angel." She waved a hand through the air. "You all think you're so wonderful! Just because you have this stupid little holier-than-thou Crowd! But thanks to Alexa, I know the truth. You," she returned her eyes to

Vivienne, "have been bad-mouthing me around school. I won't stand for it! Do you hear me?"

"I . . . I . . . have not!" Vivienne cried out. "Alexa was lying to you! But even if I had, how could you do this to me? WHO DO YOU THINK YOU ARE?! JUST BECAUSE YOU'RE BEAUTIFUL, YOU THINK YOU CAN DO ANYTHING?! YOU JOINED OUR CROWD. WE DON'T DO THINGS LIKE THIS!"

Priscilla stepped forward. She could feel the tears threatening to fall. The time had come. Finally. "And why have you been lying to us about the ties, and trying to push me out? What did I ever do to you?" It felt so good to get it out. At last.

Rebecca's smile was chilling. "Because you guys were a unit. You didn't need anyone else. And yours," she waved a hand in Priscilla's direction, "was the easiest spot to step into." She started to giggle, softly at first. "You're such an insecure mess!"

Priscilla took a step backwards. "I am? And what about you!?" she cried out before she even knew what she was saying.

And then, suddenly, Rebecca Lake, without any warning at all, began to visibly fall apart.

"YES! WHAT ABOUT ME?! YOU PEOPLE HAVE EVERYTHING!" Rebecca cried out in anguish. Tears suddenly began to spill from her eyes. "How dare you tell everyone all your crazy ideas about me! You don't know how lucky you are!"

Flabbergasted, all five girls stood in complete silence, staring at the formerly gorgeous, confident, cool, and collected Rebecca Lake . . . who was now melting away right before their eyes.

"It's not fair . . . " Rebecca continued, sobbing heavily. "You deserved it. . . ."

Instantly, Priscilla turned toward the security man, who nodded in her direction.

"All right, girls," he said calmly. "I think you can all go home." He paused for a moment. "Except for you," he nodded toward Rebecca. "I'm going to have to call your parents, dear."

"I don't have parents," Rebecca continued sobbing. "Don't you see . . . "

"Yes, you do," Gina piped up sympathetically. "You have that handsome father. . . . " She giggled nervously.

Rebecca shot her a withering look. Then, straightening her shoulders, she turned toward the security man and raised her chin in the air, tears still trickling down her cheeks. "Let's go. I've had it with all of them." She nodded toward the girls. And with that she began to walk, quickly, and with great assurance, toward the escalator.

Priscilla, Margo, Michelle, Vivienne, and Gina stood in silence as they watched Rebecca and the security man disappear.

"Well," Michelle finally sighed. "That was really something. Rebecca is like . . . like three different people." She turned to Priscilla. "How did you know? All along? She sure had me fooled. We didn't know her at all."

Priscilla shrugged. It was such a long story.

"I thought she seemed so terrific." Gina shook her head. "So beautiful and intelligent." She paused. "But, Priscilla, you knew . . . "

"What was the tip-off?" Margo asked curiously.

Priscilla hesitated. There were so many things. She was about to begin listing them when Vivienne cut in.

"Priscilla's just smart," she said simply. She turned to gaze affectionately at her friend. "And I can be a real dummy."

Priscilla half smiled, half grimaced. She turned to face her friend with a mixture of affection and anger. "To tell you the truth, Viv, I think you owe me an apology."

Vivienne bowed her head. She was quiet for a few seconds. Then she took a deep breath and let it out. "I do owe you an apology. I'm sorry. I really am." She hesitated. "Actually, though, I was right about one thing." She grinned with embarrassment. "Someone in this Crowd was insanely jealous. I just accused the wrong person."

Priscilla looked at her uncertainly. She peered around at the other Crowd members. Who?

"Rebecca." Vivienne heaved a sigh. "Don't you see? She probably wanted you out because she thought YOU were too much competition."

Priscilla stared at Vivienne blankly. Where had she heard that before?

"I did notice she was a little insensitive to you," Michelle admitted sheepishly, "but I guess I just figured she was new and a little clumsy or something."

"I'm sorry, too, Priscilla," Michelle added. "We *have* been ignoring you and the school thing. I think we got so caught up with Rebecca that it was easier just to let your problems fade." She smiled softly. "But, really, how could you have believed we'd have let anyone take your place? You should have had more faith in us" — Michelle grimaced — "even if we were all blind as bats."

Priscilla shook her head, her mother's words now suddenly resounding in her head. "The truth is, I never thought someone like Rebecca could be jealous of me." She paused. "I didn't have enough faith in me. . . . " A vision of Adam's C+ paper floated before her.

"Let's get out of here," Margo shuddered.

"I don't know," Vivienne suddenly cried out. "Do you suppose I have anything else hidden on me?" Frantically she started feeling around in her blazer, jeans, and shirt pockets while everyone began laughing.

"I don't think so," Priscilla chuckled. She grinned broadly. "Wow, it feels great being just five again."

"Yeah," Michelle nodded. "Just right."

"Almost perfect," Priscilla added.

"Why almost?" Vivienne asked with an unhappy smile. "Do I need to apologize for something else?"

"No," Priscilla grinned. "But would all of you please just take off those ties?" Her smile broadened. "If you guys want real handpainted ties, next time just come to me. . . . "

"What do you mean?" Michelle asked curiously.

"I'll explain," Priscilla smiled at her Crowd. And she would, too. Because this time they would listen.

The Practically Popular Crowd trusted her.

They respected her.

Because so did she.

20

Monday morning Alexa sat quietly at her desk, her eyes trained on the door. She could see it all now. A defeated Vivienne arriving at school, accompanied by police, or parole officers, or what have you.

The vision made her sick.

She shouldn't have just left. It was the wrong thing to do. No matter what glorious things Vivienne had been saying about Rebecca.

Speaking of Rebecca. Alexa turned around in her seat to study the empty desk behind her. Where was she?

"Hi," Vivienne's familiar voice interrupted her thoughts. Alexa whirled around to find her former closest friend settling into her seat. In her usual fashion. Knapsack to the right. Text on the desktop. She looked perfectly normal. No handcuffs.

"How are you?" Alexa asked as casually as she could.

"Fine, thanks," Vivienne answered coolly. "Why do you ask?"

"No reason," Alexa shrugged. She was dying to know. Had anything happened? Was Vivienne caught? Arrested? Did Rebecca get away?

"So where did you disappear to on Saturday?" Vivienne asked as she flipped open her history book.

Alexa cleared her throat and started rummaging through her knapsack. "I just had enough shopping."

"Well, I've had enough of Rebecca," Vivienne replied tartly. She motioned to the empty seat. "You can have her."

"No thanks," Alexa answered quickly. Too quickly. She could have kicked herself.

"I thought you were crazy about her," Vivienne responded. Slowly she turned in her seat to eye Alexa. "Exactly why did you leave Gerrards so fast? Without saying good-bye?"

"No reason," Alexa answered curtly.

"You knew," Vivienne hissed. "You knew she was shoplifting, didn't you!"

"No!" Alexa whispered back. "I mean . . . I mean what do you mean, shoplifting?"

"You heard me, Alexa Craft," Vivienne continued angrily. "You can't fool me. I know you too well. You knew, and you didn't tell us!"

Alexa looked away. "I'm not your mother. If

you're going to badmouth me in front of people, you can't expect me to stand by your side."

Vivienne stared at Alexa for an agonizingly long moment. Her eyes narrowed. "Did you know of anything else that Rebecca was up to?" she asked slowly. Accusingly.

Alexa cast her eyes downward. Innocent. She had to look innocent. "I . . . I don't know what you mean. . . . " she replied. Busily she pulled a notebook from her bag and began flipping through the pages.

"Oh, no?" Vivienne pressed on, louder now.

"Whatever are you getting at?" Alexa asked, looking up with the best imitation of confusion she could muster.

Vivienne hesitated.

Alexa breathed a sigh of relief.

Slowly, Vivienne shook her head. "I'll find out the truth one day, Alexa. I swear I will." Calmly she placed a well-sharpened pencil in the ridge at the top of her desk. "And when I do . . . "

The morning bell ripped through the air.

Alexa reached for her notebook with a shaky hand.

And when she did, Alexa would have to leave town.

Priscilla leaned casually against the hallway wall during the morning break, next to Gina and

Michelle, checking over her algebra homework. Her eyes traveled to her father's note, which was stuck to the top of the page.

You see? It doesn't matter where you learn. Just that you learn. I'm proud of you.

Gently she removed the stick-um, and smiled.

Note-writing, especially affectionate notes, was not her father's style. That made it especially nice.

"Has anyone seen Rebecca today?" Vivienne asked as she descended on the three girls.

"No," Gina shook her head. "She wasn't in our homeroom, and I haven't seen her anywhere else, either." She turned to Priscilla. "What about art? Was she there?"

Priscilla looked up at her friend and shrugged. "She wasn't. And I didn't miss her, either," she giggled.

Priscilla waved at Carol Stedman as she glided by. "See you in algebra!" She glanced at Vivienne. "Did you know Carol can speak French and Italian fluently?"

Vivienne shot Carol an admiring glance, just as Michelle appeared suddenly from around the corner.

"I just heard a rumor." Michelle lowered her voice. "Someone overheard two teachers saying that Rebecca was a very difficult girl, and that

172

her father decided to pack her off to boarding school."

Vivienne nodded with satisfaction. "Good. I hope it's on Pluto."

"Vivienne, that's not very nice of you," Gina protested. "I mean, honestly, I sort of feel sorry for her. She must be a mess inside."

"Well, you didn't have your pockets stuffed with contraband," Vivienne retorted.

Gina grimaced. "I guess that means stolen goods. Right?"

Vivienne nodded and then glanced at Priscilla. "Actually, I think we should stop talking about Rebecca altogether. Let's just consider her a bad dream. How's algebra?" She looked over Priscilla's shoulder at her homework. "EXCELLENT! Priscilla, pretty soon you'll be back with us I bet!"

Priscilla flashed Vivienne a big smile. "No thanks!"

All four girls turned to look at her with surprise.

Priscilla grinned from one to the other. "Math is just not my strong suit," she announced. "Ms. Williams' class feels good." She nodded toward her notebook sticking out from her book bag. "Now poetry is something else altogether. My poem is almost done, and it's pretty good if I do say so myself."

Suddenly, out of the corner of her eye, Priscilla spotted Adam Miller. Signaling a quick good-bye to her friends, she began moving toward him.

He smiled as she approached, and Priscilla felt a warm glow all over.

"Hi," she said almost shyly. "Still need help with your poem?"

He nodded. "I do. I've got a few lines down, but I don't know . . . " His voice trailed off dejectedly.

Priscilla slipped her arm through his. "Don't worry," she said encouragingly. "I can help."

And she could, too. What a kick. The old, the original, the in control Ms. Priscilla Levitt was positively back.

Monday afternoon Alexa was midway down the front stairs outside the school when she spotted Mac coming up toward her.

"How 'ya doin'?" he called out merrily. "I was looking for you."

"How nice," Alexa replied icily as she shot Mona a glance that said, *Don't open your mouth. Let me handle this.*

She hadn't told Mona about Rebecca's confession. It was too embarrassing.

"I was wondering if you wanted to go get a soda now or something," Mac plowed on, though it was clear he was confused by her tone. By the fact that she hadn't even stopped for a second, and had he not turned around and started trailing her, she'd have walked right past him.

"No thanks," Alexa answered matter-of-factly.

She was now at the bottom of the stairs. Finally she stopped, whirled around, and gave Mac a long, lingering, silent stare.

Then she turned to Mona. "Could you just give us a minute alone? I'll catch up."

"Sure," Mona replied quickly as she began backing off. "I'll wait on the corner."

Alone with Mac, Alexa fixed him with a big, beautiful smile. "Why don't you go look for some brunette in blue somewhere?" she asked sweetly.

"What?" Mac asked. He coughed, it seemed, nervously.

"You heard me," Alexa continued, smiling. The smiling was important. It said, you can't hurt me. You just annoy me. "A Rebecca Lake type," she added. She put one hand on her hip flirtatiously and tousled her blonde hair with the other. It was a good thing she'd worn white today. It did wonders for her complexion.

Mac nodded and looked away. He sighed and then turned back to Alexa. "Come on. Give me a break. It was just an afternoon. Besides, I mean, Alexa, we're not going steady or anything. . . . "

Alexa nodded energetically. "You got that right," she said cheerfully. "Or anything!" And with that, she turned on her heels and headed straight for Mona.

And as she did, the smile began to slip away.

Mac was awfully cute. She'd forgotten how cute.

Alexa sighed heavily. Darn Rebecca.

Mona had been right. She'd jumped into things too fast. She'd been stupid. Really dumb.

What had Mimi said this morning after Alexa had confessed the whole miserable story? Oh, yes.

"Quicksand, Lexa baby. People like Rebecca . . . they're quicksand. A person sticks their foot in just a little bit, and they get sucked right in. They don't even know what's happenin' until it's too late. . . . " She'd shaken her head. "People who cause that kind of trouble are hurtin' somewhere real bad."

Alexa rolled her eyes now. Who cared if Rebecca was miserable? She had her own problems.

"So," Mona said as Alexa arrived at her side. She waved a hand in front of her face. "Are you with me? What was that all about with Mac?"

Alexa shrugged. "I'm just not interested. I didn't want to embarrass him by saying so in front of you."

"Oh," Mona replied quietly. Diplomatically. Dubiously. "I heard Rebecca's not coming back to school," she volunteered, gamely changing the subject as they started the walk home. "Terrible."

Alexa nodded. "I did, too. Too bad."

Mona nodded somberly, and then seconds later began to chuckle. She turned toward Alexa and slipped her arm around her shoulders. "You're safe!" she cried out, her laughter growing louder now.

Alexa grinned and then, moments later, she, too, started chuckling. She was safe! Her position was secure! It was like being rescued from a molten volcano, or a life raft lost at sea, or . . .

Abruptly Alexa stopped. She looked across the street as Julia Simmons with her brand-new stylish haircut received a light kiss from Michael Phillips.

And suddenly, another thought flashed across Alexa's mind with alarming intensity.

Yes, she was safe.

But, really, for how long . . .

21

GETTING SMART

A poem by Priscilla Levitt

I yearn to be close with only a few
To know that we share the precious and new.
I yearn to feel good despite when I stumble
To know that I'm loved, even when I tumble.
I yearn for the time I spend with my art
And feel that at last I am getting smart.
For now I possess a most magical key,
It's the trust and the friend that I have in me.

About the Author

MEG F. SCHNEIDER was practically popular when she was growing up in New York City. She remembers feeling very excited and scared, insecure and confident, hurt and happy . . . sometimes all at once! And that is why she created **The Practically Popular Crowd**. She hopes it will help readers understand themselves better.

Ms. Schneider is also the author of the Apple Paperback *The Ghost in the Picture*.

She graduated from Tufts University and received a master's degree in counseling psychology from Columbia University. She lives in Westchester County, New York, with her husband and two young sons.

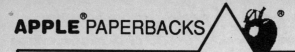

APPLE Classics

❑ MA43389-X	**The Adventures of Huckleberry Finn** Mark Twain	**$2.95**
❑ MA43352-0	**The Adventures of Tom Sawer** Mark Twain	**$2.95**
❑ MA42035-6	**Alice in Wonderland** Lewis Carroll	**$2.50**
❑ MA44556-1	**Anne of Avonlea** L.M. Montgomery	**$3.25**
❑ MA42243-X	**Anne of Green Gables** L.M. Montgomery	**$2.95**
❑ MA43053-X	**Around the World in Eighty Days** Jules Verne	**$2.95**
❑ MA42354-1	**Black Beauty** Anna Sewell	**$2.95**
❑ MA44001-2	**The Call of the Wild** Jack London	**$2.95**
❑ MA43527-2	**A Christmas Carol** Charles Dickens	**$2.75**
❑ MA45169-3	**Dr. Jekyll & Mr. Hyde: And Other Stories of the Supernatural** Robert Louis Stevenson	**$3.25**
❑ MA42046-1	**Heidi** Johanna Spyri	**$2.95**
❑ MA44016-0	**The Invisible Man** H.G. Wells	**$2.95**
❑ MA40719-8	**A Little Princess** Frances Hodgson Burnett	**$3.25**
❑ MA41279-5	**Little Men** Louisa May Alcott	**$2.95**
❑ MA43797-6	**Little Women** Louisa May Alcott	**$2.95**
❑ MA44769-6	**Pollyanna** Eleanor H. Porter	**$2.95**
❑ MA41343-0	**Rebecca of Sunnybrook Farm** Kate Douglas Wiggin	**$2.95**
❑ MA45441-2	**Robin Hood of Sherwood Forest** Ann McGovern	**$2.95**
❑ MA43285-0	**Robinson Crusoe** Daniel Defoe	**$3.25**
❑ MA42323-1	**Sara Crewe** Frances Hodgson Burnett	**$2.75**
❑ MA43346-6	**The Secret Garden** Frances Hodgson Burnett	**$2.95**
❑ MA44014-4	**The Swiss Family Robinson** Johann Wyss	**$3.25**
❑ MA42591-9	**White Fang** Jack London	**$2.95**
❑ MA44774-2	**The Wind in the Willows** Kenneth Grahame	**$2.95**
❑ MA44089-6	**The Wizard of Oz** L. Frank Baum	**$2.95**

Available wherever you buy books, or use this order form.

Scholastic Inc., P.O. Box 7502, 2931 East McCarty Street, Jefferson City, MO 65102

Please send me the books I have checked above. I am enclosing $_____ (please add $2.00 to cover shipping and handling). Send check or money order — no cash or C.O.D.s please.

Name _____

Address _____

City _____ State/Zip _____

Please allow four to six weeks for delivery. Available in the U.S. only. Sorry, mail orders are not available to residents of Canada. Prices subject to change.

AC991